MURDER
AT
SHELDON HALL

Murder at Sheldon Hall

A Reeves Giallo Detective Series

BOOK TWO

SUSAN COLLINS

A Cozy Detective Novel

Copyright © 2024
Murder at Sheldon Hall
All rights to this book are reserved, no permission is given for any part of this book to be reproduced, transmitted in any form or means; electronic or mechanical, stored in a retrieval system, photocopied, recorded, scanned, or otherwise. Any of these actions require the proper written permission of the Publishers.

Published by Birch Tree Publishing
Printed in the United Kingdom
Available at all off-line and on-line bookstores
Amazon.com and other retail outlets
ISBN: 978-1-927558-18-8
First Printed Edition, 2024

NOTE FROM THE AUTHOR

The year is 1918. The guns of the Great War have fallen silent, yet a different kind of battle rages on – one fought not in trenches, but in the grand halls of Sheldon Hall, a stately manor steeped in the shadows of loss and secrets. The echoes of conflict reverberate through its hallowed walls, intertwining with the intricate web of deceit spun by its inhabitants. This is not a tale of heroism on the battlefield, but a chronicle of human frailty and ambition, set against the backdrop of a nation grappling with the aftermath of a devastating war.

Within these pages, I present a world where the lines between right and wrong blur, where appearances deceive, and where the pursuit of justice requires more than just the observance of the law; it demands an understanding of the human heart – its capacity for both profound love and chilling betrayal. I invite you to step into the world of Charles Stow, Reeves Giallo, and the enigmatic residents of Sheldon Hall, where the only certainty is the unexpected.

Prepare to be captivated by a mystery where every clue is a carefully constructed piece in a puzzle of human desire and devastating consequences. The truth, as you will discover, is often far more complex than it initially appears.

Susan Collins

CHAPTER 1
A Soldiers Return

The train pulled into the station, its whistle a mournful cry that seemed to echo the turmoil within Charles Stow. Sheldon Hall loomed ahead, a gothic silhouette against the bruised twilight sky, its very presence a weight on his chest.

The journey had been long, the landscape blurring into a monotonous tapestry of grey fields and somber woods, mirroring the muted colours of his own mood. He'd fought in the trenches, witnessed horrors that clung to him like the mud of Flanders, yet this return felt more unsettling than any battlefield. The air here, thick with the scent of damp earth and decaying leaves, held a different kind of dread. It wasn't the immediate threat of gunfire, but the slow, insidious creep of grief and suspicion.

He'd known Thomas, his friend, for years, their bond forged in the crucible of shared youthful dreams and later, the shared horrors of war.

Now, Thomas was gone, another casualty, not of enemy fire but of a cruel twist of fate – a sudden illness that had swept him away before Charles could even say goodbye. The news had arrived as a telegram, a brittle paper announcing the end of a friendship and the start of a bewildering inheritance.

Sheldon Hall, the family estate, stood as a testament to a life lived, and now, a life ended too soon. The house itself seemed to bear the weight of Thomas's death, its stone facade stained with the shadows of the past, its windows like vacant eyes staring out at the desolate landscape. It was a place of memories, of laughter and shared secrets, now tinged with the bitter taste of loss. Even the air seemed thick with the ghosts of the past, a symphony of whispered memories and unanswered questions.

As he approached the imposing front doors, Charles ran a hand through his weary hair. The war had taken much from him; not only physical scars, but the emotional toll weighed heavily. Sleepless nights were punctuated by the recurring nightmares of the front, the screams of men lost in the mud, the ever-present threat of death. The quietude of the English countryside offered little solace. Instead, it amplified the silence, the echoing emptiness of a world stripped bare of familiar faces.

He clutched his small worn leather bag, the only possession he'd salvaged from the chaos of his departure from the war hospital. Inside, lay a few photographs of Thomas, a tattered book of poetry, and a worn letter, the last communication from his friend before his unexpected death. He hesitated for a moment at the imposing entrance of Sheldon Hall, reluctant to cross the threshold and enter the uncertain future that awaited him.

This wasn't a homecoming; it was a descent into the unknown. The butler, a tall, gaunt man named Mr. Finch, greeted him with a sombre courtesy that mirrored the overall ambiance of the estate. His eyes, like faded photographs, seemed to hold a lifetime of unspoken stories. The silence of the house was almost palpable, broken only by the rhythmic tick-tock of a grandfather clock, each second echoing the passing of time, the relentless march towards an uncertain future.

The interior of Sheldon Hall was as imposing as its exterior. The high ceilings, draped in heavy velvet curtains, seemed to absorb the remaining light of day. Dust motes danced in the faint rays that filtered through the tall, narrow windows.

Each room seemed to hold its breath, preserving the memories of generations past. The air was heavy with the scent of old wood and decaying flowers, a mixture of fragrances that spoke of both elegance and decay.

Mrs. Stow, Thomas' mother, was already awaiting him in the library. He found her sitting by a crackling fire, her silhouette stark against the flickering flames. She was a frail woman, her face etched with the lines of sorrow and worry. Her eyes, though dimmed by age and grief, still held a spark of intelligence and a hint of underlying sadness. The atmosphere in the library was heavy with unspoken emotions. He felt an instant wave of sympathy wash over him.

Their conversation was stilted, punctuated by long silences and awkward pauses. Mrs. Stow spoke of her loss, her voice trembling as she described the suddenness of Thomas's death. Charles offered his condolences, his own grief a tangible thing between them. He was here, not only as a friend mourning the loss of a comrade but as the unexpected heir to Sheldon Hall. This fact hung heavily in the air, unspoken but present, a silent specter lurking in the shadows of the grand, old library.

The following days unfolded in a monotonous blur of polite conversations and forced smiles. The estate was a place of shadows and secrets, its grandeur a deceptive facade for the underlying tensions and unspoken anxieties that simmered beneath the surface. Charles found himself increasingly isolated, a stranger in a house filled with people who seemed to regard him with a mixture of suspicion and guarded politeness.

The discovery of Lucy Stow's death was shocking and swift. It was like a scene from a horrific dream; the stillness of the morning was shattered by a scream from the housekeeper, and then a rush of horrified faces and frantic whispers. Lucy Stow, found slumped in her chair, a small, ornate vial clutched in her hand. A vial containing a lethal dose of strychnine. The scene was brutal in its stillness. The delicate porcelain teacup lay overturned on the Persian rug, its contents spilled, the tea staining the carpet a dark, brooding blot.

The silence was broken only by the erratic gasps of the housekeeper, Mrs. Periwinkle, a woman whose face had turned ashen with shock. The air reeked of fear and sudden, violent death.

Inspector Marlow, a man whose chiseled jaw seemed to clench with authority, was quick to arrive. He surveyed the scene with the cold, calculating gaze of a seasoned investigator.

His eyes, like a hawk, took in every detail, from the scattered papers on the desk to the subtle traces of spilled tea. His presence was immediately imposing, a wall of authority against the chaos. His first question, directed at Charles, was direct and accusatory.

"You are the heir, Mr. Stow. It would seem you had motive."

The question hung in the air, heavy with unspoken implications. Charles, caught in the web of suspicion, knew he needed help. He immediately contacted Reeves Giallo, a detective renowned for his unorthodox methods and his uncanny ability to unravel the most complex of mysteries. Giallo, a man as enigmatic as the mysteries he solved, had a reputation for unconventional tactics. He wasn't interested in quick arrests or superficial judgments.

His approach was one of meticulous observation and patient analysis. He would leave no stone unturned in his search for the truth. This was not a simple case of inheritance; it was a labyrinth of secrets and deception. Charles knew it, and he was desperate for Giallo's expertise.

CHAPTER 2
A Shocking Discovery

The air hung heavy with the scent of lilies and decay. Sheldon Hall, usually a testament to stately grandeur, felt suffocating, its imposing façade a grim backdrop to the tragedy unfolding within. The drawing-room, once a vibrant space filled with laughter and the clinking of teacups, was now a tableau of hushed horror. Lucy Stow lay sprawled upon a plush Persian rug, her lifeless eyes staring vacantly at the ornate ceiling. A single, delicate vial, its label long since faded, rested in her stiffened hand – a vial that held the silent, lethal whisper of strychnine.

Inspector Marlow, a man whose face seemed permanently etched with weariness, knelt beside the body, his expression a mask of professional detachment. Yet, even beneath the stoicism, Charles could sense a flicker of something akin to revulsion. The scene was stark, almost theatrical in its macabre precision. The pristine white of Lucy's lace collar contrasted sharply with the crimson stain blooming on the rug, a disturbingly beautiful contrast that spoke volumes about the brutal efficiency of the poison.

Reeves Giallo arrived shortly after, his presence a welcome counterpoint to the suffocating atmosphere. He was a study in contrasts – sharp, observant eyes that seemed to pierce through the superficial details, and an almost languid demeanor that belied his keen intellect. He moved with a quiet grace, his gaze sweeping across the room, taking in every detail, every nuance. He didn't speak, didn't offer condolences, simply began his meticulous examination.

Marlow, impatient and frustrated by Giallo's deliberate pace, cleared his throat.

"Strychnine, it seems. A clean kill, efficient. The vial was clutched in her hand, suggesting suicide. But…" he trailed off, his gaze lingering on the faint traces of a struggle – a scuff mark on the polished floorboards, a slightly askew chair, the faintest scent of something acrid mingling with the lilies.

"Suicide, Inspector?" Giallo's voice was low, almost a murmur, yet it carried a weight that cut through the silence.

He picked up the vial, examining it with a jeweller's precision. The glass was surprisingly clean, devoid of fingerprints, a detail that spoke to the killer's meticulous planning. He gently ran his thumb along the rim, tracing the almost imperceptible residue of the poison.

"I find it rather…convenient. Wouldn't you agree?"

Charles, standing silently in the background, felt the weight of suspicion pressing down upon him. He was the prime suspect, the heir apparent to Sheldon Hall and its considerable fortune. The thought was a bitter pill to swallow, especially now, amid the chilling reality of Lucy's death. He hadn't liked Lucy, not truly, but he hadn't wanted her dead. The notion of being implicated in her murder was absurd, yet the evidence, however circumstantial, seemed to point in his direction.

Giallo, his gaze shifting from the vial to Charles, let out a faint sigh.

"Let's not jump to conclusions, Inspector. A vial in her hand does not necessarily equate to suicide. Consider the possibility of it being placed there – a deliberate act of misdirection."

Marlow scoffed, his irritation growing.

"And you have a better explanation, Mr. Giallo? Perhaps the famous ghosts of Sheldon Hall decided to administer the poison?"

Giallo smiled, a thin, almost imperceptible curve of his lips.

"Ghosts are notoriously difficult to interrogate, Inspector. But humans, with their motivations and secrets, are far more interesting. Let's start with Mr. Stow. He's the obvious beneficiary, wouldn't you say?"

Charles felt a cold dread settle in his stomach. Giallo's words were true, but they felt like an accusation, even though spoken without malice. He knew he was walking a tightrope. Every word, every action, was now under scrutiny. The subsequent hours were a blur of questions, accusations, and denials. Marlow, doggedly pursuing his line of questioning, focused on the inconsistencies in Charles' alibi. He had returned from the war a changed man, haunted by the atrocities he'd witnessed. His demeanor, always reserved, had become even more withdrawn. His answers were hesitant, often punctuated by long pauses that were interpreted as guilt by the persistent Inspector.

Giallo, however, watched, observed, and listened with an almost dispassionate air. He meticulously documented every piece of evidence, meticulously cataloging the details that the less observant Inspector seemed to overlook. He examined the servants' statements, noting discrepancies in their accounts of the evening's events. He interrogated the cook, who confirmed Lucy's habit of taking her nightly tonic in the drawing-room.

He discovered a tiny scratch on Lucy's left wrist, barely visible under her lace cuff. Such an insignificant detail, easily overlooked by most, but Giallo's eye caught it instantly. As the investigation progressed, Giallo's keen intellect began to unravel the carefully constructed facade. The initial perception of a simple suicide slowly eroded as more subtle details emerged.

The precise placement of the vial, the subtle signs of a struggle, the inconsistencies in the servants' testimonies – all pointed towards something more sinister, something far more complex than a simple act of self-destruction. The discovery of a crumpled note tucked away in Lucy's desk drawer further complicated the matter. It was a hastily written note, the ink smudged and faded, but Giallo managed to decipher the message. It was a coded message, a series of seemingly random numbers and symbols. He spent hours deciphering it, his brow furrowed in concentration. The message, when finally revealed, spoke of a hidden inheritance, a secret trust fund that Lucy had established, an amount far exceeding the value of Sheldon Hall itself.

The revelation sent shivers down Charles' spine. This was more than just an inheritance; it was a web of secrets and lies. He knew he had to act fast, the net of suspicion tightening around him with every passing moment. He could only rely on Giallo, his enigmatic friend, to navigate the treacherous waters of deceit. He knew that revealing the truth would not only save him but also expose the true killer. But the question loomed: Who would risk their life for such a significant inheritance? And what was the connection between this hidden trust fund and the vial of strychnine?

The answers, Giallo knew, were concealed within the seemingly innocuous details – the scratch on Lucy's wrist, the inconsistent statements of the servants, and the coded message in the hidden drawer. The game was far from over, the truth obscured behind layers of deception and intrigue. The seemingly simple case of inheritance had transformed into a labyrinthine quest to uncover a killer, hidden within the very heart of Sheldon Hall.

CHAPTER 3
Introducing Reeves Giallo

The rain lashed against the windows of Sheldon Hall, mirroring the tempest brewing inside Charles. He paced the length of his study, the mahogany floorboards gleaming under the flickering gaslight. The weight of suspicion pressed down on him, a suffocating blanket woven from circumstantial evidence and accusatory glances. Inspector Marlow, a man whose chiseled jaw seemed to bristle with suspicion, had already hinted at arrest. Charles' inheritance, once a beacon of hope, now felt like a poisoned chalice. He needed help, and he knew exactly where to find it.

He dispatched a telegram, the crisp paper crackling in his trembling hand, the message brief but urgent: "Urgent need your assistance. Sheldon Hall…Murder…. Come at once."

He addressed it to Reeves Giallo, a man whose reputation preceded him like a shadow – a shadow that could, with skill and cunning, unveil the darkest truths.

Giallo arrived the following morning, his arrival as understated as his presence was commanding. He was a study in contrasts; a man whose sharp, observant eyes belied a quiet demeanor. His attire, a well-worn tweed suit, spoke of practicality, while the glint of steel in his gaze hinted at a mind as sharp as any blade. He wasn't tall, nor particularly imposing, but there was an aura of quiet authority that filled the room, silencing the hushed whispers of the household staff who watched him with a mixture of apprehension and curiosity. He possessed an almost unsettling stillness, a deliberate slowness in his movements that was oddly compelling. His presence was not merely felt; it was almost palpable, a tangible weight in the air.

Charles led him through the shadowed hallways of Sheldon Hall, the silence broken only by the rhythmic creak of the ancient floorboards and the mournful sigh of the wind.

Giallo didn't speak much, his gaze sweeping over every detail, absorbing the subtle nuances of the environment. He didn't need to be told about the tragedy that had befallen Lucy Stow; the atmosphere itself bore witness to it. The scent of lilies, heavy and cloying, fought with the musty odor of age and decay, creating an olfactory dissonance that reflected the emotional turmoil within the house. He observed the subtle shift in the servants' demeanor, the slight tremor in their hands, the barely perceptible flinch when he met their gaze. These were not the signs of simple grief; they suggested something deeper, a carefully constructed façade of sorrow concealing a darker truth.

They reached the drawing-room, the scene of the crime still undisturbed. The Persian rug lay crumpled, a dark stain marring its intricate design – a stain that spoke of a violent end. Giallo knelt beside the body, his examination meticulous and thorough. He touched nothing, but his eyes meticulously catalogued every detail: the slight discoloration of the skin, the subtle curvature of the fingers, the barely perceptible scratch on Lucy's wrist. Each observation was noted with the precision of a surgeon, a surgeon of the mind dissecting the intricate tapestry of a crime. He spent a considerable amount of time examining the discarded vial, its fragile glass reflecting the light, holding the potential answer to the mystery.

"Strychnine," Charles confirmed, his voice barely a whisper, the word hanging in the air like a poisonous mist. Giallo nodded, his expression betraying nothing.

He moved on, his inspection extending beyond the immediate vicinity of the body. He examined the furniture, tracing the patterns in the polished wood with a fingertip. He ran his hand over the plush velvet drapes, feeling for imperfections, hidden seams, or any indication of a struggle. He checked the fireplace, noting the carefully arranged logs, the absence of any soot or unusual ash.

He even examined the intricately patterned wallpaper, searching for any sign of tampering or alteration. His attention to detail was extraordinary, seemingly encompassing every aspect of the room, however insignificant it might appear at first glance.

He moved to the windows, carefully examining the latch, the frame, and the surrounding area for any signs of forced entry or unusual activity. He looked for fingerprints, although in this era, that science was still in its infancy. He didn't rush, his actions deliberate, almost ritualistic, each movement guided by a keen intuition honed over years of experience.

He was a silent observer, a patient hunter gathering clues from the environment, the very fabric of the room whispering secrets to his perceptive mind.

After a thorough examination of the room, Giallo addressed Charles.

"The scene has been meticulously staged," he announced, his voice low but firm. "The killer knew what they were doing."

This wasn't just a hasty crime of passion; it was a calculated act, orchestrated with precision and planning. The position of the body, the placement of the vial, even the arrangement of the furniture – all spoke of a mind intent on misdirection. He then turned his attention to the servants. He interviewed each one individually, in private, his questions precise and penetrating.

He noted inconsistencies in their accounts, subtle variations in their body language, the almost imperceptible hesitations in their speech. He observed their reactions to his questions, searching for any flicker of guilt, any sign of deception.

The housekeeper, a woman named Mrs. Periwinkle, was particularly evasive, her answers laced with carefully crafted ambiguity. The footman, a young man named Thomas, seemed genuinely distraught, but his grief lacked a certain authenticity, the depth of emotion somehow staged. The cook, a burly man with flour dusting his apron, appeared largely unmoved, his attention focused on a simmering pot rather than the dramatic events unfolding around him.

Giallo's questioning was not an interrogation in the traditional sense. He didn't shout or accuse, but he used the gentle art of suggestion, drawing information from his subjects through subtle prodding, skillfully leading them to reveal more than they intended. He noticed how Mrs. Periwinkle's eyes darted nervously towards the grandfather clock every time the subject of Timothy's whereabouts came up. A simple observation, yet it sowed a seed of doubt in Giallo's mind, fueling his investigation.

He questioned them about the intricacies of Lucy's life, probing gently for any unresolved disputes, hidden resentments, or clandestine affairs. He learned of Lucy's estranged son, Timothy, a man about whom whispers of recklessness and debt circulated within the household.

He delved into the specifics of Lucy's will, discovering a clause regarding a secret trust fund that had remained undisclosed until her death. This revelation hinted at a potential motive far greater than simply inheriting the estate.

The investigation wasn't confined to interviews and observation. Giallo meticulously examined Lucy Stow's personal belongings, searching for clues hidden in plain sight. He found a hidden compartment in her writing desk, revealing a collection of coded letters, their meaning encrypted behind an intricate cipher. He spent hours deciphering the cryptic messages, slowly unraveling a web of deceit far more complex than initially perceived.

He meticulously reconstructed Lucy Stow's final movements, piecing together a timeline from fragments of information gathered from the servants' testimonies and his own observations. He examined Lucy's schedule, scrutinized her appointments, and investigated her social interactions in the days and weeks leading up to her demise.

He found a pattern, a subtle but significant recurring theme in Lucy's activities and interactions. A carefully constructed web of relationships and alliances, woven together to support the killer's plan. His sharp mind worked relentlessly, piecing together the fragments of information like a master craftsman assembling a delicate mosaic. The image slowly emerged, a picture of calculated betrayal, meticulously plotted and flawlessly executed. The more he investigated, the more intricate the scheme became, the deeper the rabbit hole extended. The case that appeared at first glance to be a simple inheritance dispute transformed into a complex tapestry of deceit, woven with strands of betrayal and hidden ambitions.

Days turned into nights as Giallo delved deeper into the mystery. The imposing structure of Sheldon Hall seemed to loom over him, its shadows and secrets whispering tales of intrigue and betrayal. The rain continued to batter the windows, a rhythmic accompaniment to the relentless pace of his investigation. His work was far from over. The truth remained elusive, hidden behind layers of deception and intrigue.

Yet, Giallo, with his sharp mind and unwavering determination, was determined to uncover it, no matter how deep the darkness might reach. The path to justice would be long and arduous but Giallo was ready to traverse it. The hunt had begun.

CHAPTER 4
Timothy

The flickering gaslight cast long shadows across Timothy Stow's gaunt face. He sat hunched in a worn armchair by the fireplace in the drawing-room, a half-empty glass of brandy clutched in his hand, its amber liquid mirroring the unsettling hue of his eyes. He hadn't slept properly in days, the weight of his mother's death pressing down on him like a physical burden. The accusation, though unspoken, hung heavy in the air, a palpable presence that clung to him like the damp chill of the autumn evening.

Giallo watched him, his keen eyes assessing every twitch, every nervous shift of posture. Timothy was a study in contrasts: his expensive, if slightly faded, clothing spoke of a past elegance, while his current dishevelled appearance hinted at a life unraveling. There was a haunted look in his eyes, a mixture of grief and something else – a simmering resentment that Giallo found both intriguing and unsettling. He had initially been considered a mere peripheral figure in the investigation, a grieving son caught in the whirlwind of his mother's sudden demise. But Giallo sensed there was more to Timothy than met the eye.

His alibi, for instance, was remarkably weak. He claimed to have been at the local pub, "The Crooked Tankard," but the landlord, a portly man with a suspicious squint, couldn't definitively recall seeing him. His testimony was vague, hazy with the fog of alcohol and the passage of time. The rain that night had been torrential, making accurate recollections difficult, yet the lack of concrete corroboration was a significant red flag.

Giallo had spent the better part of the day piecing together Timothy's recent life. He learned of significant gambling debts – a staggering sum for a man of his apparent means. He'd fallen into arrears with several creditors, his once-comfortable lifestyle threatened by mounting financial pressures. The pressure had become intense in the last few months, with several increasingly aggressive dunning letters from creditors discovered amongst his mother's correspondence. One particularly vicious one, with threats of legal action, had been delivered just three days before Lucy Stow's death. This was certainly a strong motive. Could desperation have driven him to such a desperate act?

Beyond the financial struggles, there was a more complex relationship with his mother. Giallo learned through discreet inquiries amongst the household staff that their relationship had been strained for years. Lucy Stow, a woman of considerable strength and independent spirit, had disapproved of Timothy's lifestyle, constantly clashing with him over his reckless spending and his aversion to responsibility. She had been the sole provider, supporting his life of indolence and gambling habits, and although he had received some minor income from investments, he hadn't done much to increase that. Her disapproval hadn't been subtle; it was a cold, calculating disdain that permeated their interactions, creating a constant undercurrent of resentment. The staff had recounted several heated arguments, some bordering on violence, in the weeks leading up to her death.

These clashes were not merely squabbles between mother and son; they were battles for control, a power struggle fueled by financial dependence and simmering animosity.

Yet, there was another side to their complex dynamic. Giallo discovered through conversations with the housekeeper, a woman named Mrs. Periwinkle who had served the Stow family for over thirty years, that Lucy Stow possessed a deep, if often frustrated, love for her son. Mrs. Periwinkle spoke of her mistress's hidden generosity, of quiet acts of support that Timothy seemed to carelessly disregard. There were instances of seemingly unpayable debts mysteriously settled, of unexpected financial windfalls that appeared just when Timothy was on the brink of ruin. These acts of kindness, however, were never accompanied by open affection or approval. Lucy Stow's love was a complex, contradictory emotion – a mixture of fierce loyalty and exasperated disappointment.

This conflicting relationship added another layer of complexity to Timothy's case. Could a son, burdened by debt and resentment, yet still bound to his mother by a twisted form of familial loyalty, have been capable of such a crime?

It was a question that gnawed at Giallo. He delved into the details of Lucy's will, scrutinizing every clause, every carefully chosen word. The document was impeccably drafted, leaving no room for ambiguity. The bulk of the estate, including Sheldon Hall, was bequeathed to Timothy.

This seemingly straightforward arrangement, however, raised a disturbing question in Giallo's mind: what if Timothy had already received enough money to solve his financial woes, either from his mother or from another source? If he had obtained this support, then the substantial inheritance might become less vital, yet still have a tempting effect. The motive would change; from desperation, his actions might have been spurred by greed instead.

Giallo's investigation took him beyond the confines of Sheldon Hall, into the murky underbelly of the local gambling dens and loan sharks' offices. He unearthed a network of shady dealings and illicit transactions, tracing Timothy's debts back to a particularly ruthless moneylender known only as "Silas." Silas, a man with a reputation as cold and calculating as the winter winds that whipped across the Yorkshire moors, remained elusive. Giallo had to approach carefully; a direct confrontation would risk alerting Silas to the investigation.

Giallo also investigated the details of Timothy's life prior to his mother's death. There was a pattern of impulsive behaviour, interspersed with periods of withdrawal and despondency. He was a man teetering on the precipice of ruin, his life a precarious balancing act between extravagant spending and desperate attempts to recover his financial standing. The constant pressure might have pushed him to a breaking point, to a desperate act fueled by desperation or perhaps a cynical attempt to solve his mounting debts, his future possibly looking brighter by claiming the inheritance.

The intricacies of Timothy's character continued to confound Giallo. Was he a cold-blooded killer driven by greed, or a desperate man pushed to the edge by his own recklessness?

Was his seemingly frail alibi a result of a genuine lack of recollection or a carefully constructed deception? The truth, as Giallo suspected, was likely far more nuanced, a tangled web of financial desperation, familial tension, and perhaps, a streak of unexpected ruthlessness hidden beneath a veneer of outward fragility. The rain continued to fall outside, a constant, mournful reminder of the storm that had broken over Sheldon Hall and its inhabitants. Giallo, however, remained undeterred, his determination fueled by the intricate puzzle that lay before him, a puzzle where every piece, however seemingly insignificant, held the key to unlocking the truth.

The hunt for the truth was far from over, and Timothy Stow remained firmly in his sights, a suspect whose ambiguous character presented a complex challenge to unravel. The next step was to find Silas. Only then might the full extent of Timothy's involvement – or lack thereof – become clear.

CHAPTER 5
Inspector Marlow's Hasty Conclusion

The rain, a relentless percussion against the leaded windows of Sheldon Hall, seemed to mirror the relentless drumming of Inspector Marlow's impatience. He paced the length of the drawing-room, his polished boots clicking a counterpoint to the crackling fire. Timothy Stow, still slumped in the armchair, remained an unnerving enigma. The brandy snifter sat untouched now, its amber contents a forgotten detail in the larger drama unfolding. Marlow, a man of routine and procedure, found himself profoundly unsettled by the ambiguities that Giallo, his far less orthodox counterpart, seemed to revel in.

"The evidence is overwhelming, Giallo," Marlow declared, his voice sharp and clipped, the words echoing the sharp angles of his jawline.

"The son, inheriting the estate, a strained relationship with the mother, a lack of alibi—it all points to Timothy." He stopped pacing, hands clasped behind his back, the picture of assured authority. He might have been a stern schoolmaster delivering a final judgment rather than a detective piecing together a complex case.

Giallo, seated comfortably on a nearby settee, regarded Marlow with his usual calm detachment. The firelight danced in his dark eyes, revealing a glint of amusement that Marlow found both irritating and perplexing.

"Overwhelming, Inspector? Or merely convenient?" Giallo's voice was soft, a counterpoint to Marlow's harsh pronouncements, yet it carried an undeniable weight. Marlow bristled. "Convenient? The woman was poisoned, Giallo. Strychnine, a swift and brutal end. And who benefits most? Her son, the one burdened by debt, the one with a questionable past, the one without a credible alibi for the night of her death. The pieces fit together too neatly, don't you think?"

"Neatly arranged, perhaps," Giallo countered, a subtle shift in his tone. "But arranged by whom, Inspector? Are we to assume that every circumstantial detail, every seemingly incriminating piece of evidence, is automatically the truth? Or might some of these so-called 'facts' be… manipulated?"

Marlow scoffed.

"Manipulated? By whom? Ghosts? The rain? We're dealing with a murder, not a gothic novel."

His disdain was palpable, a mixture of irritation and a deep-seated belief in the sanctity of procedure. He believed in facts, in tangible evidence, in the straight forward application of the law, and Giallo's subtle insinuations felt like an affront to his established world view. He saw Timothy Stow as the perfect embodiment of a villain straight from a penny dreadful. A weak, indebted, and morally questionable son; the classic archetype of the murderer. It was a narrative that suited Marlow's methodical mind, a narrative that neatly tied up the loose ends of the case.

"The war has left many men changed, Inspector," Giallo observed, his gaze drifting towards the rain-lashed windows. "Many with debts, many with secrets. Many susceptible to desperation. Timothy's circumstances, while certainly…problematic, don't automatically translate to guilt."

Marlow frowned. Giallo's words, though seemingly innocuous, were carefully chosen barbs aimed at the heart of Marlow's hasty conclusions. He saw only the surface, the convenient narrative that fit neatly into his worldview, overlooking the intricate tapestry of human motivations and deception that Giallo seemed to effortlessly decipher.

"Desperation doesn't usually involve strychnine, Giallo. This was calculated, precise. A professional's work, perhaps. Someone who knew what they were doing, someone with a specific intent. And who else had the opportunity, the means, and the motive?"

Marlow's voice rose slightly, his frustration simmering. Giallo's unconventional approach threatened to unravel Marlow's carefully constructed narrative.

Giallo leaned forward, his voice dropping to a near whisper.

"And what of the motive, Inspector? We assume greed. But is it so simple? Greed is a powerful motivator, yes, but are we overlooking other possibilities? Perhaps bitterness, resentment, a carefully cultivated sense of injustice? Perhaps a conspiracy far more intricate than we can initially perceive?"

Marlow shifted his weight, the silence stretching between them, thick with unspoken accusations and simmering resentment. The clash of their methodologies was stark – Marlow's reliance on tangible evidence and swift judgment versus Giallo's more nuanced approach, his willingness to delve into the murky depths of human psychology.

Marlow, a product of a rigid, war-torn society, valued order and efficiency above all else, finding comfort in the familiar and the predictable. Giallo, scarred by the war's chaotic realities, understood that the truth was seldom straightforward, often hidden beneath layers of deception and obscured by human complexities.

To Marlow, Timothy Stow was the obvious culprit – a weak man driven by avarice, a convenient fit for the stereotypical criminal profile. Giallo, however, saw a far more complex individual, a man whose fragility might hide a deeper truth, or perhaps, be a carefully crafted deception.

"Inspector," Giallo said softly, breaking the tension. "We have barely scratched the surface of this investigation. While Timothy Stow's circumstances certainly make him a suspect, we must exhaust all avenues before we reach a conclusion. Rushing to judgment serves only to obscure the truth."

Marlow remained unconvinced, his gaze fixed on Timothy, who sat silently observing the exchange with a chilling blend of detachment and barely concealed anxiety. The weight of suspicion, fuelled by the inspector's unwavering belief in his guilt, hung heavy in the air, an unspoken accusation that seemed to solidify Timothy's position as the prime suspect in Marlow's mind.

Yet, Giallo's words, though subtle, planted a seed of doubt, a crack in the edifice of Marlow's hasty conclusion. The game of deduction had begun, a battle of wills and methods played out against the backdrop of a rain-swept manor, where the truth remained elusive, masked by layers of deceit and half-truths. And beneath the surface of Marlow's unwavering certainty, a flicker of uncertainty began to ignite. The meticulously arranged pieces of the puzzle, initially so perfectly aligned in his mind, now seemed to shift and rearrange, their arrangement no longer so neatly obvious.

The doubt, once imperceptible, began to grow, challenging his assumptions, forcing him to confront the possibility that his meticulously constructed narrative might just be a mirage, cleverly designed to conceal the true killer. The relentless rain outside seemed to amplify the weight of this growing uncertainty. The storm outside mirrored the storm brewing within Marlow himself.

The silence hung heavy in the air, punctuated only by the crackling fire and the rhythmic drumming of the rain. Marlow finally broke the silence, his voice devoid of its earlier confidence.

"Very well, Giallo. But we need to find Silas. His testimony could be crucial."

He looked at Timothy, his expression less accusatory, yet still tinged with suspicion.

"For now, Mr. Stow remains a person of interest." The unspoken caveat – that he remained the most likely culprit in Marlow's mind, even with his acknowledgement of the need for further investigation – hung in the air. The Inspector, despite the seed of doubt planted by Giallo, clung to his preconceived notions. He allowed himself a momentary pause, a subtle shift in his stance. He conceded the need for further investigation, yet his gaze remained fixed on Timothy, a silent affirmation of his lingering suspicions. The battle between the two detectives was far from over, a silent clash of ideologies waged within the shadowed walls of Sheldon Hall.

The following days were a blur of interviews, interrogations, and the painstaking examination of seemingly insignificant details. Marlow, despite his initial certainty, found himself increasingly frustrated by the lack of concrete evidence directly linking Timothy to the crime. Giallo, on the other hand, seemed to thrive on the ambiguity, pursuing leads that Marlow dismissed as irrelevant or inconsequential. He spent hours poring over old ledgers, examining the intricate financial dealings of the Stow family, uncovering a trail of hidden debts, clandestine transactions, and carefully concealed resentments.

He interviewed servants, neighbors, even the local postman, seeking any shred of information that could shed light on the hidden complexities of the case.

Marlow watched Giallo's methods with a mixture of disdain and grudging admiration. Giallo's intuitive approach, his uncanny ability to discern the truth beneath the surface, was frustrating to Marlow, a man who relied on established procedures and tangible evidence.

Yet, the meticulous nature of Giallo's investigations, his unwavering pursuit of the truth, slowly began to chip away at Marlow's entrenched beliefs. He couldn't deny the increasing evidence of a deeper, more sinister plot unfolding. The meticulous nature of the poisoning, the calculated placement of the incriminating evidence, all suggested a level of sophistication that far exceeded Timothy's capabilities.

The search for Silas continued. He was a shadowy figure, a former employee of the Stow family, rumored to have known Lucy's secrets. His disappearance added another layer of complexity to the already tangled web of deceit. Giallo's relentless pursuit led him to a forgotten corner of the estate, a dilapidated stable where he uncovered a hidden compartment containing a cache of letters. These letters revealed a secret affair, a hidden inheritance, a web of financial entanglements that far exceeded the initial assumptions. The letters spoke of betrayal, ambition, and a carefully orchestrated plan to frame an innocent man.

As Giallo pieced together the fragmented truths revealed in the letters, the pieces of the puzzle began to fall into place, creating a picture far different from the one Marlow had initially envisioned. The truth, far from being simple and straightforward, was a complex tapestry of deceit, hidden motives, and clandestine relationships. Timothy Stow, it turned out, was a pawn in a far larger game, a victim of a carefully orchestrated conspiracy designed to secure a vast inheritance for someone else entirely. The carefully constructed facade of guilt that had initially convinced Marlow began to crumble, revealing the intricate machinations of those who pulled the strings from the shadows. The rain had finally stopped. The sun, breaking through the clouds, cast a brilliant light on the truth, revealing a hidden world of secrets and betrayal.

The truth, Giallo knew, was not always what it seemed. And in the case of Lucy Stow's death, it was far more convoluted and sinister than anyone could have imagined.

CHAPTER 6
Giallos Initial Investigation

The chill October air bit at Giallo's cheeks as he surveyed Sheldon Hall. The imposing manor, shrouded in a perpetual twilight even under the pale sunlight, seemed to exude an aura of unspoken secrets. Inspector Marlow, with his brisk efficiency and air of self-importance, had already declared the case closed, pointing a finger at Timothy Stow, the deceased's son. But Giallo, his keen eyes missing nothing, felt a prickle of unease, a discordant note in the symphony of presumed guilt. Marlow's hasty conclusion, built on flimsy evidence and societal biases, felt… incomplete.

Giallo's investigation began not with grand pronouncements or dramatic interrogations, but with the meticulous observation of detail. He moved through the sprawling house like a phantom, his footsteps barely audible on the thick carpets. The crime scene, Lucy Stow's study, was already largely undisturbed, the police having completed their initial sweep. Yet, Giallo found himself drawn to the seemingly insignificant. The slight displacement of a book on the shelf, the faint smudge of a foreign substance on the highly polished writing desk, the barely perceptible scuff mark on the antique Persian rug near the fireplace – these were the whispers Giallo sought to decipher.

He began with the vial of strychnine, the supposed murder weapon. Marlow had dismissed it as straight forward: a suicide. But Giallo, holding the tiny glass bottle in his gloved hands, noted the lack of fingerprints, the almost pristine condition of the stopper, and the strangely dry residue inside. This wasn't the careless act of a desperate woman; it was a staged scene, carefully orchestrated to mislead.

His trained eye caught the faintest trace of a different chemical compound, a residual scent that defied simple explanation. He carefully collected a sample, noting its coordinates within the study for his later analysis.
Next, he turned his attention to the witnesses. Charles Stow, the prime beneficiary of Lucy's will, was a puzzle wrapped in an enigma. His grief seemed genuine, but beneath the veneer of sorrow, Giallo sensed a carefully constructed facade. Charles' wartime experiences, the trauma he had endured in the trenches, were etched onto his face, a permanent reminder of the horrors he had witnessed. Yet, his demeanor held a disconcerting calmness, a detachment that felt unnatural, given the circumstances.

The interview with Charles was a delicate dance, a careful exploration of his movements on the day of the death. Giallo observed Charles' subtle shifts in posture and his slight hesitation when he spoke of his time in the study that morning. The man was withholding something, a fact that was reinforced by his evasive responses and the controlled way in which he answered Giallo's questions. His calm exterior was a deliberate attempt to mask something far more sinister.

Emily Grace, Charles' enigmatic cousin, proved to be even more elusive. Beautiful, intelligent, and with an almost unnerving composure, she possessed an air of quiet confidence that belied a deep-seated mystery. Her interactions with Charles were laced with unspoken understanding, a shared secret that hung heavy in the air between them. Her alibi, a visit to a nearby village, seemed plausible on the surface, yet Giallo sensed a carefully woven fabrication in her narrative. He questioned the timeline of her movements, noting discrepancies in the timings she provided and the details she omitted.

The housekeeper, Mrs. Albright, a woman weathered by years of service, provided a different perspective.

Her account of the household dynamics painted a picture of simmering resentment and long-held grudges. She spoke of the strained relationship between Lucy and Timothy, the financial difficulties Timothy faced, and the palpable tension between Charles and Emily, a tension that transcended mere familial friction. Mrs. Albright's words, delivered in a quiet voice, held the weight of years of unspoken observations.

Timothy, the initial prime suspect, proved to be an enigma within an enigma. He possessed a quiet dignity that belied his troubled past. While his behavior seemed erratic and his alibi questionable, Giallo noted the genuine anguish in his eyes. The young man seemed genuinely distraught by his mother's death. His financial problems were genuine, documented by his bank statements, but this did not automatically translate into a motive for murder. Giallo felt certain that the initial rush to judgment was erroneous.

Giallo's attention turned to the will. Lucy Stow's testament was a masterwork of legal obfuscation, deliberately designed to complicate matters. While it favored Timothy, various clauses and contingencies created a complex web of potential beneficiaries, leaving ample room for legal battles and manipulation. This intricacy pointed towards a calculated plan, perhaps even a deliberate attempt to create a chaotic aftermath. The will itself was a clue, meticulously crafted to serve a hidden purpose.

As Giallo delved deeper into the family history, he uncovered a rich tapestry of hidden resentments and long-standing feuds. The Stows weren't just a family; they were a battlefield of unspoken grievances and simmering ambitions. The estate itself, Sheldon Hall, seemed to echo the discord, its grandeur masking a legacy of betrayals and broken trust.

Each room held a silent testament to the family's history, whispers that Giallo diligently pieced together.
He spent hours in the estate library, poring over old journals and family correspondence. He unearthed letters revealing past disputes over land, money, and inheritance. These letters illuminated the complex relationships within the family, revealing long-standing rivalries and hidden desires. The seemingly trivial details acquired significance as Giallo woven them into his comprehensive narrative.

Days bled into nights as Giallo relentlessly pursued his investigation. He meticulously documented his findings, cross-referencing information, analyzing statements, and seeking out inconsistencies. He was not merely collecting facts; he was constructing a narrative, a story that revealed the intricate web of deceit woven around Lucy Stow's death.

He was not merely a detective; he was a historian, meticulously piecing together the fragments of a shattered life. The picture he was beginning to assemble was far more complex, and sinister, than anyone had initially imagined. The truth, he felt, was a hidden jewel, buried beneath layers of deception and carefully constructed lies. And he was determined to unearth it, no matter the cost.

CHAPTER 7
Emily Graces Introduction

The flickering gaslight cast long shadows across the polished mahogany desk in Giallo's modest York lodgings. He steepled his fingers, the faint scent of pipe tobacco mingling with the sharper aroma of old paper and ink. The case of Lucy Stow's death, initially appearing straightforward, had unravelled into a Gordian knot of deceit, each thread leading to a new labyrinth of suspicion. Inspector Marlow, with his characteristic bluster and a healthy dose of self-satisfaction, had declared the case closed, pinning the blame squarely on Timothy Stow. But Giallo, ever the pragmatist, found himself increasingly uneasy. There were too many loose ends, too many inconsistencies, too many silences. His thoughts returned to Sheldon Hall, its imposing silhouette looming against the backdrop of the bleak autumnal sky. The house itself seemed to hold its breath, a silent accomplice to the tragedy within its walls. The servants, their faces etched with a mixture of fear and suppressed gossip, had offered little in the way of concrete information. Their reticence, Giallo surmised, was a testament to the power dynamics at play within the Stow family, a power that had ultimately led to Lucy's demise.

Then there was Charles Stow, the heir apparent, his grief a carefully constructed façade that Giallo found increasingly unconvincing. Charles' demeanor shifted from a display of inconsolable sorrow to a calculated composure, a transformation so abrupt that it raised more questions than answers. His attempts to appear distraught seemed too meticulously rehearsed, too strategically performed. Giallo had noted the subtle twitch in his left eye, a barely perceptible tremor that betrayed his carefully constructed mask of grief.

It was during his meticulous review of Lucy Stow's financial records that the name Emily Grace first caught his attention. It wasn't a name directly associated with the Stow family, at least not in the official records. Yet, there were several cryptic entries in Lucy's ledger, coded transactions disguised as household expenses, amounts far exceeding what would be expected for ordinary household maintenance. These transactions, Giallo realized, were linked to a series of coded messages, almost indecipherable, penned in a barely legible script. He spent days deciphering the coded entries, the process a frustrating exercise in patience and deduction.

Each successfully decoded entry revealed a small piece of the puzzle, a piece which gradually brought into focus a figure he'd initially overlooked: Emily Grace. Emily Grace was Charles Stow's cousin, a woman shrouded in mystery. She was rarely mentioned in conversations with the household staff, her existence relegated to hushed whispers and furtive glances.

Yet, her presence at Sheldon Hall was undeniable, evidenced by the sporadic entries in the ledger, the hushed conversations overheard by the housekeeper, and the faint scent of her unique perfume—a blend of lavender and sandalwood— lingering stubbornly in the library. Giallo realized she was more than a peripheral figure; she was a key player in this unfolding drama.

He obtained a photograph of Emily Grace from an old family album he found tucked away in the attic of Sheldon Hall. She was a striking woman, with fiery red hair cascading down her shoulders, striking green eyes that seemed to pierce through the veil of deception. Her features were sharp, her expression intense, her mouth hinting at a quick wit and an even quicker temper.

There was a quiet strength about her, a hint of defiance in the set of her jaw that suggested a woman who was used to getting her own way, a woman who wouldn't hesitate to manipulate those around her to achieve her goals.
His investigation into Emily Grace led him to a small, almost forgotten village nestled in the remote countryside. The village was quaint, filled with half-timbered houses and cobblestone streets, but the local gossip was far from quaint. The villagers spoke of Emily Grace in hushed tones, describing her as a woman of sharp intellect and questionable morality, a woman known for her captivating charm and her ruthless ambition.

One old woman, her face a roadmap of wrinkles, confided that Emily was "as sharp as a serpent and twice as dangerous."
He learned that Emily had a history of financial dealings of a dubious nature. There were rumours of risky investments, questionable partnerships, and even whispers of involvement in illegal activities before her sudden disappearance from the village several years earlier. This information, while not directly implicating her in Lucy Stow's murder, painted a picture of a woman capable of deception and ruthlessness.

Returning to York, Giallo compared his findings with the coded messages from Lucy Stow's ledger. The entries revealed a complex financial scheme involving Emily, Charles and a network of seemingly unconnected individuals. The transactions were meticulously disguised, each entry serving as a coded message, a cryptic breadcrumb in a trail of deceit. It was a testament to Emily's cunning that she managed to maintain such a low profile, her involvement hidden behind a veil of secrecy and carefully placed misinformation.
The messages, once deciphered, revealed a network of illicit transactions, shadowy deals that involved significant sums of money.

The money appeared to have been laundered through a series of shell corporations, carefully concealing the true source of the funds. Giallo realized that Lucy Stow was not simply a wealthy widow; she was at the centre of a sophisticated web of financial intrigue. The money, Giallo suspected, was the motive behind Lucy's death. But the question remained: who wanted her dead, and why?

As Giallo pieced together the puzzle, he began to suspect a deeper connection between Charles and Emily. The coded messages hinted at a clandestine relationship, a partnership born out of shared ambition and a thirst for wealth. Their supposed grief for Lucy seemed almost perfunctory, a calculated performance designed to deflect suspicion. The meticulously orchestrated alibi, the carefully planted evidence pointing to Timothy – it all pointed to a collaborative effort, a joint conspiracy.

He recalled a seemingly insignificant detail from his earlier visits to Sheldon Hall – a single, crimson hair found clutched in Lucy Stow's hand. It was too long and too vibrant to belong to Lucy, and it certainly wasn't Charles.' It was a shade of red that matched perfectly with the vivid red hair in Emily Grace's photograph. This small detail, overlooked by Inspector Marlow in his rush to judgment, became a crucial piece of the puzzle.

The truth, Giallo realised, was not a simple case of murder for inheritance. It was a complex tapestry of greed, ambition, and betrayal, woven with threads of carefully concealed transactions and expertly crafted lies. It was a testament to the cunning of Charles and Emily, a testament to their ability to manipulate events and mislead those around them. They had used their intimate knowledge of Lucy's financial dealings, their shared understanding of her vulnerabilities, and their meticulous planning to frame Timothy, exploiting the loopholes in the legal system to achieve their aims.

The picture was becoming clear. Charles, driven by his desperation to secure the Stow family fortune, had formed a pact with his enigmatic cousin. Emily, with her business acumen and her ruthless ambition, provided the intelligence and the execution.

Their plan was audacious, risky, and brilliantly conceived – a masterpiece of manipulation that had almost succeeded. But Giallo, with his unwavering dedication to truth, was about to unravel their web of deceit, revealing the chilling truth behind the death of Lucy Stow, and the shocking secret alliance that lay at its heart. The game, Giallo knew, was far from over. The final act was about to begin.

CHAPTER 8
Unraveling Alibis

The scent of woodsmoke and damp earth clung to Giallo's coat as he left Sheldon Hall, the chilling November air biting at his cheeks. Marlow's hasty conclusion, the arrest of Timothy Stow, felt like a premature victory, a closing of the book before the final chapter had even begun. Giallo knew better. The intricate dance of deception, the carefully laid trap, was too elegantly woven to be dismissed so readily. He needed to delve deeper, to dissect the alibis, to unearth the inconsistencies that Marlow, in his rush to judgment, had overlooked.

His first target was Timothy. The young man's alibi for the night of his mother's death hinged on his claimed presence at the village pub, The Crooked Tankard. He'd sworn to have been there from seven until closing time, a solid six hours. But Giallo, ever the meticulous investigator, had already begun his own discreet inquiries. He found the pub's barmaid, a stout woman with shrewd eyes and a surprisingly sharp memory, distinctly hesitant when questioned about Timothy's presence. Her initial affirmation, delivered with a touch of forced enthusiasm, wavered under Giallo's gentle, probing questions.

She admitted to serving Timothy a single pint of ale, but couldn't recall him beyond that. The other patrons, who had been questioned by the local constable, corroborated her vague recollection; a fleeting image in the smoky haze of a busy evening. The time frame was entirely too short for an alibi supposedly spanning six hours. Giallo noted this carefully. A single pint scarcely constituted an alibi. A man capable of murder wasn't likely to linger in a public house for hours if he had recently poisoned his mother.

This discrepancy, small though it seemed, cast a long shadow over Timothy's account. Then there was Emily Grace, Charles' enigmatic cousin. Her alibi was even more meticulously crafted, seemingly airtight.
She had claimed to have spent the evening at her own cottage, a modest dwelling nestled a mile from Sheldon Hall.

She claimed to have been occupied with meticulous needlework, preparing a wedding sampler, a task that demanded unwavering concentration. The local vicar, a portly man with a penchant for gossip, confirmed that she had indeed spent a significant portion of the evening at her cottage. He'd observed her through the window, he claimed, a comforting sight given the dark and stormy night.

But Giallo remained skeptical. The vicar's testimony, while seemingly credible, lacked specificity. He couldn't offer precise timings, and the details of his observations were disappointingly vague. Giallo's investigation shifted from questioning witnesses to a meticulous forensic analysis of Emily's alibi. He obtained a warrant to search her cottage. The room was immaculately tidy, the sampler half-finished, the needle resting perfectly on the fabric. But Giallo's keen eyes noticed subtle anomalies. The faint scent of almonds, a tell-tale sign of cyanide, lingered faintly in the air. A trace amount, barely detectable, but enough to raise suspicion.

His examination of the sampler revealed that the embroidery was astonishingly precise for someone allegedly working for hours in the weak light of an oil lamp. This perfection suggested that the intricate design, rather than being painstakingly completed in a single, long session, could have been done in short bursts, interspersed with other activities. The timing was crucial. His next move was to examine the circumstances under which the poison might have been administered.

Strychnine, a particularly potent poison, left little trace in the stomach, a detail Inspector Marlow had somehow overlooked. It required careful calculation and timing to administer a lethal dose without arousing suspicion. The question was not whether the poison was administered at the Hall, but when. Lucy Stow, it seemed, was not the target of a single, sudden strike. Her death might have been the culmination of a prolonged scheme.

Giallo recalled Lucy Stow's routine. She was a woman of habit, a creature of routine. Her day always started with a glass of warm milk, a habit that had been confirmed by the household staff. Giallo suspected that the strychnine might have been introduced into the milk over a period of days, a slow accumulation of the poison disguised within the familiar comfort of her morning beverage. This gradual poisoning explained the lack of immediate symptoms, the absence of any violent struggle that would have been expected in the event of a sudden, large dose.

The intricacies of the case unraveled further. He then revisited the letters and documents found in Lucy Stow's possessions. A seemingly innocuous note, overlooked by Marlow, caught Giallo's attention. It was a brief correspondence between Lucy and her lawyer detailing the process of creating the revised will; the one that disinherited Timothy. A single misplaced comma, discovered through careful scrutiny of the original draft, suggested that the exact wording of the bequest had been altered subtly, the change introduced sometime after Lucy's initial instructions. The change was so subtle as to be nearly invisible but it was enough to shift the inheritance from Timothy to Charles if no other heir could be found. This minor alteration pointed to a scheme that had been in progress long before Lucy's death.

He focused then on Charles' alibi. Charles claimed to have spent the evening working on his war-related paperwork.

But a meticulous search of Charles' room in the manor revealed a number of discrepancies. The work was incomplete, the papers scattered haphazardly across the table. A careful analysis of the ink showed that it was not the same ink Charles usually employed. Moreover, several crucial documents, which Charles claimed to have examined were conspicuously absent. These discrepancies, while seemingly insignificant in isolation, pointed to a fabricated narrative.

The papers weren't merely disordered; they were meticulously arranged to appear chaotic, a deliberate attempt to convey the impression of diligent work. The evidence pointed towards a concerted effort to construct a plausible alibi. Giallo decided to confront Charles directly. He outlined the inconsistencies discovered, and the implications of this false alibi. The facade of innocence that Charles maintained faltered under the weight of Giallo's evidence. Charles' demeanor shifted, the calm composure crumbling under the strain of his carefully constructed lies.

The fear in his eyes confirmed Giallo's suspicions. He was guilty. Not of directly poisoning Lucy Stow, but of being a willing accomplice in a meticulously planned scheme that cost her life. Emily, too, crumbled under pressure. Confronted with the findings, her air of self-assurance evaporated. The intricate needlework, the seemingly perfect alibi, were all part of a grand deception. Both Charles and Emily were skilled manipulators, adept at weaving a web of lies to conceal their actions. They had used their knowledge of Lucy's routine, their understanding of human nature, to create a scenario that seemed plausible, almost airtight. But Giallo's relentless pursuit of truth, his meticulous attention to detail, had exposed the flaws in their carefully constructed plan.

The truth, when it finally emerged, was far more complex than the simple narrative of murder and inheritance. It was a story of greed, ambition, and a chilling pact forged in the shadow of war. The motive was not simply money, but a power play, a desperate gamble to secure a future amidst the uncertainty of a world torn apart.

Charles' love for Emily, rather than driving him to act out of passion, had instead fueled a cold, calculating ambition. Their love was intertwined with a ruthless plan, a testament to the darker side of human nature. They had exploited the law, using the uncertainty and chaos of wartime to their advantage. And in the end, their intricate plot was undone not by force, but by the quiet, determined persistence of a man who believed in truth.

CHAPTER 9
The Will and the Inheritance

The solicitor, a Mr. Finch, a man whose face seemed perpetually etched with the weariness of dealing with the affairs of the deceased, arrived at Sheldon Hall the following morning, clutching a worn leather briefcase. He was a small man, almost swallowed by his oversized coat, his movements hesitant, as if he feared disturbing the stillness of the house that held a recent tragedy. He presented the will with a somber flourish, the parchment crisp and brittle, yellowed with age, bearing the elegant, looping script of Lucy Stow.

Giallo, ever observant, noted the faint tremor in Finch's hand as he placed the document on the table. He had witnessed similar tremors before, the subtle betrayals of a man burdened by secrets or a conscience weighed down by uneasy truths. The will, however, was anything but simple. It was a labyrinth of clauses and stipulations, a testament to Lucy Stow's shrewdness and perhaps, a hint of her own carefully constructed deceptions.

The initial clauses were straightforward enough. Specific bequests were made: a collection of antique porcelain dolls to a distant niece, a prized Persian rug to a local church, various smaller items distributed amongst the household staff. These provisions, Giallo surmised, were designed to appear as acts of generosity, softening the harsh reality of the more substantial dispositions to follow.

Then came the crux of the matter, the allocation of the Sheldon Hall estate and its considerable wealth. The will stated that the main portion of Lucy Stow's substantial fortune, including the Hall itself, was to be inherited by her son, Timothy, provided he reached the age of thirty without having been found guilty of a felony.

This was a significant condition, especially given Timothy's current predicament. The provision was clearly intended to safeguard the inheritance from potential legal challenges, even indirectly acknowledging the suspicion surrounding him.

A subtle but crucial clause followed, adding a layer of complexity to the already intricate arrangement. If Timothy were to die before reaching the age of thirty, or if the felony condition were ever met, the inheritance would be divided equally between two parties: Charles Stow, Lucy's late friend's son, and Emily Grace, Charles's cousin. This detail provided a significant motive for any party involved to ensure that Timothy never achieved the age threshold, thus triggering the alternative inheritance clause.

Further adding to the intrigue, a smaller but not insignificant trust fund was established for Emily Grace, regardless of the outcome regarding the main inheritance. This provision suggested a preferential treatment towards Emily, raising questions about Lucy's relationship with her granddaughter. Had there been a closer bond between them than previously apparent? Or was this a deliberate attempt to manipulate events in a way that benefited Emily? The financial implications were staggering.

Sheldon Hall wasn't just a stately home; it was a vast estate encompassing hundreds of acres of prime farmland, valuable timberlands, and lucrative mineral rights. The fortune attached to it was substantial, even by pre-war standards. To inherit it would mean financial security, social standing, and the power that accompanied both. The will, therefore, wasn't just a legal document; it was a battleground, a carefully drawn map delineating the potential rewards and the devastating consequences for those embroiled in this complex game of inheritance. Giallo studied the document meticulously, his eyes tracing every word, every comma, every carefully placed phrase.

He saw the legal precision, the calculated ambiguity, the subtle hints of manipulation. He realized that Lucy Stow was not simply a victim; she was a player, a master strategist who had meticulously crafted her own posthumous power play, setting the stage for a deadly drama even from beyond the grave. The will became less a document of inheritance and more a complex puzzle piece in the unfolding mystery of her death.

The document offered a new perspective on the motive behind the murder. If Timothy were eliminated, both Charles and Emily would inherit significantly. The division would be equitable, but if Timothy were never eliminated, both would eventually lose their chance at the inheritance due to the time constraints of the will.

However, this implied a greater level of collaboration between Charles and Emily than initially suspected. It spoke of a carefully orchestrated plan, a cold-blooded conspiracy hatched in the shadows. Giallo's mind raced. Had Charles and Emily conspired to eliminate Timothy, knowing that the will provided them with a lucrative alternative? This notion fit with the evidence of manipulated alibis and planted clues discovered earlier. The timing was impeccable – the murder occurring just days before Timothy would have passed the crucial age limit specified in the will. This wasn't just a simple murder; it was a calculated financial manoeuvre, a deadly game of inheritance played with the stakes impossibly high.

The will, however, also contained a clause that was curiously ambiguous. It mentioned a "secret codicil," a supplementary document attached to the original will, which was to be opened only in specific circumstances. The conditions of opening were opaque at best; all it mentioned was to be opened if the primary inheritor were deemed legally unfit to inherit.

The conditions were deliberately vague and likely were meant to cause confusion that could be manipulated depending on circumstances. The absence of clear information only fueled Giallo's suspicions. Was this codicil the key to the entire mystery? Did it contain some crucial information that would shed light on the true perpetrators, or did it contain further twists and turns, leading down another rabbit hole? This would become another point that Giallo needed to investigate urgently. The will, therefore, wasn't merely a legal document, but rather a roadmap to the truth, guiding his investigation deeper into the heart of this web of deceit.

The weight of the evidence, combined with the intricacies of Lucy Stow's will, shifted the focus of the investigation. The initial suspicion surrounding Timothy was now considerably less convincing. Instead, the spotlight fell squarely on Charles and Emily, their meticulously planned actions painting a chilling portrait of ambition and cold-blooded calculation. The will wasn't just a document of financial arrangements; it was a blueprint of their conspiracy, a testament to the lengths they were willing to go to secure their fortune.
The subtle nuances of the will – the conditional clauses, the hidden codicil, the careful distribution of smaller bequests –painted a picture of Lucy Stow's shrewdness and cunning.

She had anticipated potential challenges, carefully constructing a legal document that could be manipulated to suit the desires of those she deemed worthy or unworthy of her fortune. Had she suspected treachery within her own family? Or was this a calculated gamble, a game played even after her death?
Giallo realized that the will wasn't just a testament to her wealth; it was a mirror reflecting her own complex character, a window into the shadowy machinations of those vying for her inheritance.

It was a document filled with layers of legal complexities, ambiguities, and possible manipulations, offering further clues to the unfolding mystery. The will itself had become a weapon, a tool utilized in this deadly game of deception, revealing that Lucy Stow's death was not just a tragic accident, but a meticulously orchestrated plot, where the lines between victim and perpetrator were hopelessly blurred.

The discovery of the will, therefore, was not merely a procedural step in the investigation but a pivotal moment that changed the course of the entire case. It had provided Giallo with the key to unlock the true motive and identity of Lucy Stow's killer. The seemingly straightforward case of murder and inheritance had evolved into a sophisticated game of manipulation, where the stakes were high, the players cunning, and the truth hidden beneath layers of carefully constructed deceit. The investigation was far from over; in fact, it had only just begun to unveil its true complexity.

The path towards justice was now clearly defined, leading to the heart of a web of lies and betrayal, woven with the threads of ambition, greed, and a love as dark as the secrets it concealed. The game, Giallo knew, had only just begun.

CHAPTER 10
Hidden Motives Emerge

The solicitor, Mr. Finch, had departed, leaving behind a lingering scent of old paper and the unsettling quiet that followed the revelation of Lucy Stow's will. Giallo, however, felt anything but quiet. The will, while seemingly straightforward in its distribution of assets, had only served to deepen the mystery surrounding her death. The initial assumption of a simple inheritance-driven murder now felt simplistic, almost naive. There was a complexity to the Stow family, a web of unspoken resentments and simmering tensions that hinted at a far more intricate motive.

He began his deeper investigation by revisiting the seemingly insignificant details. He spent hours poring over the family's old correspondence, letters yellowed with age and brittle with time, their ink faded but their words still whispering secrets. He discovered a pattern of strained relationships, a history of simmering rivalries and bitter disagreements that had been carefully concealed beneath a veneer of polite society.

Timothy Stow, initially the prime suspect due to his suspicious behavior and lack of alibi, emerged as a figure shrouded in more complexities than initially perceived. While his actions were certainly questionable, Giallo found evidence suggesting he was a man burdened by a deep-seated sense of inadequacy. His letters to his mother revealed a yearning for her approval, a constant struggle to meet her expectations, a struggle that seemingly never brought him any satisfaction. He was not the cold, calculating killer Inspector Marlow perceived; rather, a man desperate for love and acceptance, a desperate craving possibly exploited by more ruthless individuals.

The letters also revealed a complex relationship with his aunt, Emily Grace, Charles Stow's cousin. Their correspondence, while initially seemingly innocent, revealed a subtle undercurrent of resentment and unspoken competition. Emily, a woman of sharp intelligence and considerable ambition, possessed a fierce independence that clashed with the traditional expectations of women in her social circle. She had always been overshadowed by Lucy, her aunt, and harbored a deep-seated jealousy of her position and influence within the family. This jealousy, Giallo suspected, might have played a significant role in the events leading to Lucy's death.

Then there was Charles Stow himself. While he had initially seemed to be merely a beneficiary of the will, his own correspondence revealed a darker side. He expressed, in coded language, an almost obsessive desire for wealth and status, a deep-seated insecurity masked by a veneer of charm and affability. His letters revealed not only his love for Emily Grace, but also an alarmingly pragmatic approach to obtaining his desires, one that bordered on ruthlessness. The carefully constructed facade of grief he presented to the world crumbled beneath the weight of Giallo's investigation.

Giallo's investigation delved into the intricacies of the Stow family history, uncovering old property disputes, bitter inheritance battles, and long-forgotten scandals. He learned of a clandestine affair Lucy Stow had engaged in decades prior, an affair that had resulted in a child born out of wedlock, a child never acknowledged by the family. This child, now grown, held a potential claim to the Stow fortune, a claim that could have dramatically altered the dynamics of the inheritance, a piece of the puzzle he had overlooked.

Further investigation led Giallo to uncover a series of secret meetings held within the shadowy corners of Sheldon Hall. These meetings, attended by various members of the Stow family, suggested a conspiracy that ran far deeper than the apparent motive of inheritance. He found cryptic notes, hidden compartments in old desks, and secret passages within the sprawling manor house, all hinting at a conspiracy so complex it could challenge even the keenest intellect.

He discovered that Timothy, in his desperation to please his mother, had been unwittingly used as a pawn in a larger game of manipulation. Emily, fuelled by resentment and ambition, had skillfully played on his vulnerabilities, using his lack of confidence and desire for his mother's approval to orchestrate events to her advantage. Charles, with his ruthless ambition and deep-seated desire for wealth, had played the role of the grieving friend, meticulously crafting an alibi while secretly orchestrating events from behind the scenes.

The hidden resentment within the family stemmed from more than just monetary gains. It was a tapestry woven from years of suppressed emotions, unmet expectations, and long-held grudges, culminating in the tragic demise of Lucy Stow. Each family member had their own secret motives, their own hidden desires, and their own contributions to the complex web of deceit that surrounded her death.

As Giallo pieced together the fragments of evidence, a chilling narrative emerged. It was a story of ambition, betrayal, and the destructive power of long-held resentments. The will, far from being a straightforward document, was a catalyst, the spark that ignited a long-simmering powder keg of family tensions. The struggle for wealth was only the superficial layer of the conflict.

Beneath lay a complex interplay of familial relationships, intertwined with secrets, lies, and unspoken desires that had festered for years. The investigation led Giallo into the dimly lit corners of York's high society, a world of hushed whispers, clandestine meetings, and carefully guarded secrets. He delved into the past, uncovering old scandals and forgotten betrayals, each piece of information adding another layer of complexity to the case. He discovered that Lucy Stow's seemingly idyllic life had been far from peaceful; she had spent years battling with various members of her family, each dispute adding more fuel to the already simmering tensions.

The exploration of the family dynamics revealed a startling truth about human nature. It demonstrated how greed and ambition could twist even the closest familial bonds, turning loved ones into bitter enemies. The seemingly straightforward case of murder had evolved into a profound exploration of human nature, a tapestry woven with threads of envy, resentment, and a desperate hunger for power. Giallo understood that this case was not just about finding a killer; it was about understanding the intricate motivations that drove people to commit such heinous acts.

The meticulous piecing together of the evidence, the examination of the family dynamics, the reconstruction of events—all of it pointed towards a motive far more profound than mere inheritance. It was a motive rooted in years of suppressed resentment, simmering jealousies, and the desperate craving for approval, all brought to a head by the catalyst of Lucy Stow's death. Giallo began to see a picture not of a simple murder, but of a meticulously orchestrated plan that had been years in the making, a plan so intricate and so carefully constructed that it almost succeeded in concealing the truth.

The true nature of the crime, he realised, lay not in the act itself, but in the intricate web of relationships and hidden motives that had led to it. The investigation was far from over, and the path towards justice was fraught with even more unforeseen twists and turns, as he delved deeper into the heart of the Stow family's dark secrets. The game, it seemed, was only just beginning to reveal its true complexity.

CHAPTER 11
Planting the Seeds of Doubt

The rain hammered against the leaded windows of Sheldon Hall, mirroring the turmoil brewing within its walls. Charles Stow, still pale from his war wounds, sat by the fire, his gaze fixed on the dancing flames. He'd known Lucy Stow for years, a kind woman, if a little eccentric. Her death, so sudden, so violently unnatural, left a bitter taste in his mouth.

He felt the weight of suspicion, a heavy cloak clinging to him, the chilling gaze of Inspector Marlow a constant presence in his mind. He shifted uncomfortably, the stiffness in his war-injured leg a physical manifestation of the unease that gnawed at him. Across the room, Emily Grace, his cousin, sat embroidering, her needle flashing in the firelight. She, too, possessed an air of quiet unease, a barely concealed tension that betrayed her calm exterior.

Their stolen glances, fleeting moments of shared understanding, spoke volumes, though neither dared to utter the unspoken words hanging heavy between them. The unspoken words: their secret, the carefully constructed web of deceit they had woven together, the threads of which now threatened to unravel.

Their conversations were laced with veiled meanings, subtle cues only they could understand. He'd mention the intricate workings of the old clock in the hall, a device he'd examined closely, its inner mechanisms mirroring the complex machinations of their plan. She'd respond with a seemingly innocuous comment about the dampness affecting the library's books, a reference to the very place where they'd planted a crucial piece of false evidence – the now-infamous vial of strychnine.

Their shared secret, their forbidden love, was the foundation upon which their scheme rested. It had begun as a desperate attempt to secure financial stability, a means to escape the shadows of poverty and the uncertainty of the post-war world. But the seed of their ambition had blossomed into something far darker, far more dangerous. The inheritance, initially seen as a lifeline, had become an obsession, a powerful force that twisted their desires and warped their morals.

Charles, haunted by the horrors he'd witnessed on the battlefield, saw in Lucy's death a chance for redemption, a way to create a future free from the constraints of his past. The trauma he'd endured had left him emotionally scarred, prone to impulsive decisions, yet capable of chilling calculation. His meticulous nature, honed by years of military precision, had served him well in constructing the intricate plot to incriminate Timothy.

Emily, ever the pragmatist, saw the financial security the inheritance offered as a shield against a bleak future. She had always been ambitious, a sharp mind veiled beneath a facade of demure femininity. She possessed a keen understanding of human nature, a skill she'd used to manipulate those around them, subtly planting seeds of suspicion and doubt wherever they were needed.

Her social graces masked a steely resolve, her calm exterior hiding a passionate heart capable of great cruelty. Their discussions, seemingly casual, were peppered with veiled references to their plan, a secret language understood only by them. The innocuous question about the gardener's whereabouts, the seemingly accidental mention of Timothy's gambling debts, the casual observation about the placement of certain objects – each detail was carefully chosen, a piece in their intricate game of deception.

They had meticulously crafted a narrative that pointed towards Timothy's guilt, exploiting the existing tensions within the family, playing upon the Inspector's prejudices and his eagerness to secure a quick arrest. They knew Timothy's weaknesses: his gambling addiction, his volatile temperament, his strained relationship with his mother. They'd used these vulnerabilities against him, planting the seeds of suspicion subtly and skillfully.

The vial found clutched in Lucy's hand was not an accident; it was a deliberate act, a carefully staged piece of evidence. The strychnine itself was obtained through clandestine channels, a testament to their planning and resourcefulness. They'd even gone to the lengths of forging a series of letters suggesting a financial dispute between Timothy and his mother, exacerbating already existing familial friction.

The meticulous nature of their deception was evident in every detail. They understood the legal system, knew its strengths and weaknesses, and they exploited those weaknesses ruthlessly. They had studied the concept of double jeopardy, recognizing it as a potential shield against further investigation if their initial plan went awry. Their plan was not born of impulse, but of meticulous calculation.

It was a complex tapestry woven from threads of deceit, carefully concealed beneath a veneer of normalcy.

Their actions were not fueled solely by greed, but by a twisted sense of love and desperation. Their relationship, born in secrecy, bound them together in a desperate pact for survival.

They saw themselves as victims of circumstance, forced into a desperate act to secure a better future. This shared trauma, this warped sense of shared destiny, formed the dark heart of their conspiracy.

But their carefully constructed facade was beginning to crack.

Reeves Giallo, with his keen intellect and his methodical approach, was steadily unraveling their lies, exposing the inconsistencies, the carefully planted red herrings, the subtle manipulations. The weight of their deception was pressing down on them, their carefully constructed world teetering on the brink of collapse. The rain outside intensified, mirroring the gathering storm of their impending downfall.

The tension between Charles and Emily thickened, a silent acknowledgement of the encroaching danger. Their glances were no longer filled with the conspiratorial intimacy of shared secrets, but with a growing apprehension. Their meticulously constructed plan, once a source of perverse satisfaction, now felt like a suffocating weight, threatening to crush them beneath its burden. The quiet moments were laced with unspoken anxieties, the shared burden of their lie a tangible presence between them. Their whispers, once conspiratorial and hushed, were now strained and tense. They exchanged worried glances, their faces etched with the strain of their deception. They had played a dangerous game, a game with high stakes, and now the consequences threatened to overwhelm them.

As the days turned into nights, the tightening net of Giallo's investigation cast a long shadow over their existence. The subtle questioning, the scrutinizing gaze, the careful scrutiny of their every word and action – all contributed to a growing sense of dread. The quiet elegance of Sheldon Hall, once their sanctuary, had become a suffocating prison. The cracks in their charade were becoming increasingly visible, threatening to expose the dark truth beneath. The burden of their deceit, once shared, was now beginning to fracture their bond, the stress of their carefully constructed lie driving a wedge between them.

The seeds of doubt, so carefully planted to incriminate Timothy, were now beginning to sprout within their own hearts. The rain continued to lash against the windows, a relentless accompaniment to their growing fear. The game was far from over, and the final act was about to begin.

CHAPTER 12
Exploiting the System

The flickering firelight cast long, dancing shadows across Charles's face, highlighting the grim determination etched into his features. He'd always considered himself a pragmatist, a man of action, but this... this intricate web of deceit he'd woven with Emily felt alien, a monstrous creation that threatened to consume him. He'd justified it, of course. Lucy's fortune was rightfully his, he'd argued; Timothy, with his flighty ways and questionable habits, would only squander it. But the escalating stakes, the constant fear of exposure, were eroding his resolve.

Emily, usually so composed, paced the room like a caged animal. The meticulously crafted façade she'd maintained throughout the investigation was beginning to crumble. The initial plan had been elegant in its simplicity: leverage Timothy's inherent recklessness, plant enough circumstantial evidence to cast suspicion, and let the legal system do the rest. Double jeopardy, that hallowed principle of English law, was their ultimate safeguard. Once Timothy was acquitted, or even if the case faltered and the charges were dropped, he could never be prosecuted again for the same crime. The beauty of their scheme lay in its apparent infallibility.

Their strategy had involved several key elements. First, they'd subtly manipulated Timothy's already erratic behavior. Charles, feigning concern, had 'loaned' Timothy significant sums of money, knowing his penchant for gambling. He'd seen to it that these transactions were subtly documented, leaving a paper trail that could be misinterpreted as desperation and financial duress.

Simultaneously, Emily, using her charm and social connections, had spread whispers of Timothy's gambling debts, his supposed desperation, and his increasingly erratic conduct. These rumours, planted like carefully cultivated seeds in the fertile ground of local gossip, began to blossom into a narrative of a man pushed to the brink.

The next stage had been the planting of evidence. Charles, using his knowledge of the house and Lucy's routines, had strategically placed several crucial pieces of "incriminating"evidence. A partially burned letter, suggesting Timothy's desperation and a potential motive, was discovered amongst Lucy's papers. A pawnbroker's receipt, ostensibly showing Timothy pawning family heirlooms to settle his debts, was strategically left in plain sight. Each piece of evidence, seemingly insignificant on its own, contributed to a powerful, damning narrative.

"The Inspector is growing suspicious, Charles," Emily said, her voice tight with anxiety. The carefree confidence she'd displayed earlier was gone, replaced by a palpable fear.

"His questioning was sharper this morning. He seems to be focusing more on the inconsistencies in Timothy's story, not the evidence itself."

Charles clenched his jaw. He'd underestimated Inspector Marlow's tenacity. The man was a bulldog, relentless in his pursuit of the truth.

"We need to be more careful. Our actions need to be consistent with our narrative. Any further slip-up could unravel everything."

Their carefully constructed alibi had been another key component of their scheme. Charles had used his war injuries as a convenient excuse for his limited movements on the night of Lucy's death, claiming he'd been too unwell to leave his room. Emily, as a devoted cousin, had corroborated his story, painting a picture of devoted care.

Their plan hinged on the seamless alignment of their accounts, a coordinated performance aimed at diverting suspicion away from them. They had even rehearsed their lines countless times, ensuring consistency and precision.

But a growing unease began to creep into their meticulously crafted plan. The pressure of maintaining their charade, the fear of discovery, was becoming unbearable. The weight of their secret was beginning to fracture their bond, the constant fear driving a wedge between them. Their previously effortless collaboration was now fraught with tension, their interactions laced with suspicion and distrust.

The meticulously detailed ledger, detailing the movement of money, the careful placement of false clues, the manipulation of witnesses – it all seemed monstrously calculated now, in the cold light of their growing fear. The rain outside continued to lash against the windows, a relentless, rhythmic pounding that mirrored the frantic beating of their hearts.

Their carefully constructed alibi, built on lies and deception, was starting to fray at the edges. The Inspector's growing suspicion was a constant, unsettling presence, a dark shadow looming over their carefully constructed reality. The slightest misstep, the smallest inconsistency, could unravel their entire plan, exposing their dark secret to the harsh light of day. The letter, the pawnbroker's receipt, the subtly manipulated testimony – each piece of evidence, carefully planted, now felt like a potential landmine, ready to explode beneath their feet. The fear was palpable, clinging to them like a shroud. They were trapped in a web of their own making, the threads tightening with each passing moment.

The weight of their guilt was becoming almost unbearable. The meticulously crafted plan, once a source of perverse pride, now felt like a suffocating burden, threatening to crush them under its weight.

The moral compass, which they'd so easily disregarded in pursuit of their avarice, was now a sharp, accusatory finger pointing at their hearts.

The growing tension between Charles and Emily was a reflection of the cracks appearing in their meticulously crafted deception. Their once-seamless collaboration was now fraught with mistrust and suspicion, each interaction laced with a barely concealed animosity. The seeds of doubt, meticulously sown to incriminate Timothy, were now sprouting within their own minds, undermining their carefully constructed narrative. The rain continued its relentless assault on the windows of Sheldon Hall, the rhythmic drumming a relentless counterpoint to their growing despair. The game, they both realised, was far from over. The final act was about to begin, and the curtain was about to rise on a scene far more terrifying than either of them had ever imagined.

The very system they had so cleverly manipulated was now poised to expose their crimes, to drag them into the harsh light of justice. The fear, cold and clammy, gripped them both, a chilling reminder of the precariousness of their position, and the devastating consequences that awaited them. They had played a dangerous game, and now they were about to pay the price. The meticulously crafted web of deceit, so cleverly spun, was finally starting to unravel, threatening to expose the dark truth beneath, a truth that would shatter their lives forever.

CHAPTER 13
The Weight of Evidence

The Inspector, a man whose face seemed perpetually etched with the weariness of a thousand unsolved cases, leaned back in his chair, steepling his fingers.

"The strychnine, found in the remains of her teacup," he began, his voice a low rumble, "was a clear indication of murder. The timing, the lack of forced entry... it all pointed to someone within the house." His gaze drifted towards Charles, lingering for a moment before moving on to Timothy, who sat rigidly in his chair, his knuckles white as he gripped the arms. Giallo, however, remained silent, his keen eyes meticulously scanning the room, taking in every detail, every nuance of expression. He knew the Inspector was relying heavily on circumstantial evidence, a dangerous path in a case as complex as this. The initial assumptions, Giallo believed, were built on a foundation of sand, ready to crumble under the weight of a thorough investigation.

"Inspector," Giallo finally spoke, his voice calm but firm, a stark contrast to the charged atmosphere of the room, "with all due respect, I believe we've been focusing on the wrong details. The crime scene, while seemingly straightforward, presents some intriguing inconsistencies." He began to unravel the thread of his argument, his words carefully chosen, each phrase a carefully placed stone in the edifice of his counter-argument.

"The teacup, for instance. While traces of strychnine were indeed found, the concentration was surprisingly low. Low enough, in fact, to suggest the poison might have been diluted, perhaps accidentally, or perhaps... intentionally."

This subtle suggestion hung in the air, a seed of doubt planted in the Inspector's mind. Giallo continued, his voice gaining momentum, "And the tea itself? The Inspector's report mentions a faint, almost imperceptible, scent of almonds. A detail, perhaps, that was overlooked in the initial assessment. Yet, almonds, or rather, bitter almond extract, is often used as a masking agent for the taste of strychnine. This suggests a certain level of sophistication on the part of the killer, someone with some knowledge of poisons and their effects."

He paused, letting his words sink in, before continuing,

"Furthermore, the supposed lack of forced entry is questionable. The windows, as I observed, showed signs of recent cleaning, almost too meticulous for a casual glance. This implies an attempt to erase any trace of forced entry, a deliberate effort to mislead the investigation. It was a clever touch, designed to point suspicion towards an insider."

Timothy, previously rigid, shifted slightly in his chair. A flicker of hope, barely perceptible, crossed his face. Charles, however, remained impassive, his expression unreadable, a mask of carefully controlled emotions. Giallo moved on to the statements of the suspects.

"The Inspector's report relies heavily on the statements provided by both Charles and Timothy. Yet, upon closer examination, discrepancies emerge. For instance, Timothy's account of his movements on the night of the murder contains inconsistencies, minor details that seem insignificant on the surface but, when viewed in conjunction with other evidence, suggest a carefully constructed alibi."

He leaned forward, his gaze sharp and unwavering.

"Charles's statement, while appearing plausible, lacks the emotional depth one would expect from a man grieving the loss of a close friend and potential benefactor. His detachment is almost... too perfect. A carefully rehearsed performance, designed to deflect suspicion?" The Inspector, his skepticism slowly giving way to thoughtful consideration, tapped a pen against his notepad.

"You're suggesting a conspiracy, Giallo? That the evidence, the statements, were manipulated?"

"Precisely, Inspector," Giallo affirmed, his voice calm and measured. "I propose a scenario where the killer, possessing knowledge of poisons and forensics, meticulously staged the crime scene to direct suspicion towards a convenient scapegoat. Someone with a motive strong enough to risk everything, and the intelligence to cover their tracks effectively. Someone who understood the intricacies of the law, and the concept of double jeopardy."

He turned to Timothy, a hint of compassion in his eyes.

"Mr. Stow," he said softly, "I believe you were framed. Your apparent guilt was meticulously crafted, a piece of theatre designed to conceal a far more sinister plot." Giallo then proceeded to elaborate on the details. He described the careful placement of the teacup, the subtle use of the almond extract, the meticulous cleaning of the windows, all orchestrated to create a false narrative. He presented evidence that the initial forensic examination had missed crucial details: microscopic traces of soil on Timothy's shoes that didn't match the grounds of Sheldon Hall, but aligned perfectly with a secluded path leading to a nearby quarry, a path known only to a select few.

He detailed how the timings of Timothy's movements, while seemingly incriminating, allowed for sufficient time to establish an alibi and then return to the scene undetected. The supposedly missing evidence, Giallo argued, hadn't been missed; it had been deliberately hidden in plain sight.

He explained how the narrative of Timothy's supposed guilt had been skillfully woven into the initial investigation, using the existing biases and assumptions to solidify the Inspector's belief in Timothy's guilt. This was more than just a crime; it was a masterful manipulation of the justice system, a game played on the very principles of law and order. Giallo then delved into Lucy Stow's financial affairs, revealing a complex web of investments and hidden assets.

The discovery of a hidden compartment in her desk, concealed behind a loose brick, revealed documents outlining substantial debts, debts that could have driven someone to desperate measures.

The weight of the evidence shifted, subtly at first, then with increasing force. The Inspector, initially resistant, found himself grudgingly acknowledging the flaws in his initial assessment. The carefully constructed case against Timothy was beginning to crumble, revealing the cracks in the seemingly solid foundation upon which it rested. Giallo continued his methodical exposition, patiently dismantling the carefully constructed façade of circumstantial evidence. He dissected each piece of evidence, revealing the deliberate manipulations, the cleverly hidden clues, and the subtle inconsistencies that painted a different picture.

He highlighted the improbabilities, the contradictions, and the deliberate omissions in the initial investigation. The meticulous reconstruction of the events surrounding Lucy Stow's death painted a picture of cold calculation and cunning deception, where seemingly minor details played a crucial role in misdirecting the investigation.

The deliberate planting of false evidence, the carefully orchestrated alibis, the calculated manipulation of witnesses—all pointed towards a far more intricate and sinister plot than anyone had initially anticipated.

The atmosphere in the room thickened, heavy with the weight of revelation. The Inspector's initial confidence was replaced by a growing sense of unease. His gaze shifted from Timothy, now visibly relieved, to Charles, whose impassivity finally began to crack, revealing a flicker of something akin to fear.

Giallo's presentation was a masterclass in deduction, a compelling narrative weaving together seemingly disparate pieces of evidence to expose a truth hidden beneath layers of deceit. The intricate web of lies, so carefully spun, was finally unraveling, revealing the true perpetrators behind Lucy Stow's murder, and the chilling motive behind their heinous crime. The weight of the evidence, once pointing overwhelmingly towards Timothy, now lay heavily on the shoulders of those who had so skillfully manipulated the system. The truth, as Giallo so meticulously revealed, was a far more complex and unsettling affair than anyone could have imagined. The final pieces of the puzzle were now falling into place, ready to expose the darkest secrets of Sheldon Hall.

CHAPTER 14
A Confrontation with Marlow

The air in Marlow's office hung thick with the scent of stale tobacco and unspoken accusations. Giallo, ever the picture of controlled intensity, leaned against the desk, his gaze unwavering as he met Marlow's steely stare. The Inspector, a man whose face seemed permanently etched with the lines of countless unsolved cases, remained seated, his expression a mask of professional skepticism. The silence stretched, punctuated only by the rhythmic ticking of a grandfather clock in the corner, each tick a hammer blow against the fragile peace.

"Inspector," Giallo began, his voice a low, measured counterpoint to the clock's insistent rhythm, "I believe your conclusions regarding young Timothy are… premature." Marlow grunted, a non-committal sound that spoke volumes. He'd built his career on concrete evidence, on irrefutable facts, and Giallo's insinuations felt like a personal affront.

"Premature? The evidence points directly to him, Giallo. The strychnine, the lack of alibi, his suspicious behaviour… it all adds up."

Giallo smiled, a slow, deliberate curve of his lips that betrayed none of the turmoil brewing beneath the surface.

"Indeed, Inspector, it appears to add up. But appearances, as you know, can be deceiving. A carefully constructed illusion, perhaps?"

He paused, allowing his words to hang in the air, to sink into the Inspector's hardened resolve. He then launched into a meticulous deconstruction of the case, a methodical dismantling of Marlow's assumptions. He began with the strychnine, questioning the purity of the sample, suggesting the possibility of contamination, a subtle detail easily overlooked in the rush to judgment.

He pointed out the inconsistencies in the testimonies of the house staff, the subtle discrepancies in their accounts that, while seemingly insignificant individually, painted a larger picture of orchestrated confusion.

"Consider the alibi, Inspector," Giallo continued, his voice gaining momentum. "Timothy claims he was in the village, but no one corroborates his story. Convenient, isn't it? But is it proof? No….It's a lack of evidence, not evidence of guilt."

He paced the small confines of the office, his movements precise and purposeful, each step a calculated maneuver in a silent battle of wits.

He then turned his attention to the most damning piece of evidence — the proximity of Timothy to the scene of the crime.

"The Inspector's focus has been primarily on Timothy's presence near the scene of the crime, overlooking a far more crucial aspect. While his presence may seem incriminating, was it not precisely because he was expected to be there? A carefully crafted deception, allowing for a swift and convenient scapegoat."

Marlow, visibly irritated, shifted in his chair.

"You're suggesting a conspiracy, Giallo? That someone framed Timothy?"

"Precisely, Inspector. A conspiracy so intricate, so meticulously planned, that it almost fooled you."

Giallo produced a worn, leather-bound notebook, its pages filled with his meticulous notes and sketches. He opened it, revealing a series of interconnected diagrams, each one a piece of the intricate puzzle he had painstakingly assembled.

"Observe," Giallo said, pointing to a specific entry. "This letter, discovered hidden within Lucy Stow's personal effects, reveals a secret, a motive far more compelling than mere inheritance disputes. It outlines a clandestine affair, a betrayal, a network of tangled

relationships driven by avarice and deceit."
He explained the contents of the letter, revealing a web of hidden desires and secret alliances that had been masked by a carefully constructed facade of respectability. He meticulously laid out how the letter provided a credible motive, exposing a financial scheme far more elaborate and dangerous than anyone had initially imagined. The letter exposed a plot to secure a substantial inheritance through murder, and the manipulation of the justice system. This plot was meticulously executed, framing Timothy in a way that seemed almost foolproof.
The Inspector leaned forward, his skepticism slowly melting away in the face of Giallo's undeniable evidence.

The contrasting investigative styles of the two men highlighted the tension in the room; Marlow, a man of procedure and concrete evidence, and Giallo, a master of deduction and the subtle art of observation. Marlow, trained in the rigid structure of police procedure, found himself grappling with a reality far more nuanced and complex than he had initially anticipated. His belief in the straightforward justice system was challenged by Giallo's intricate revelations, a sophisticated web of deception that transcended the simplicity of a single suspect.

"The letter," Marlow murmured, tracing a finger across the page, "it changes everything." His gaze shifted to the intricate diagrams, his eyes following the flow of Giallo's reasoning. He studied the evidence, carefully re-evaluating the information, as each piece of the puzzle fell into its proper place, revealing the depth of the conspiracy. He saw the subtle manipulations, the calculated misdirections, the skillful weaving of a web of deceit that had almost trapped him. Giallo continued, explaining how Charles Stow, ostensibly a grieving friend, had orchestrated Timothy's downfall, exploiting the existing tension within the family and utilizing the prevailing societal biases of the time to create an environment conducive to deceit and manipulation. He detailed Charles' relationship with Emily Grace, Charles' cousin and a key player in the conspiracy, highlighting their shared motive and their meticulous planning. He described how they had meticulously planted false evidence, manipulated witnesses, and exploited the weaknesses in the legal system to achieve their goals.

"They counted on the double jeopardy law, Inspector," Giallo said, his voice low. "To ensure that Timothy would never be tried again, no matter what new evidence surfaced."

Marlow leaned back, the weight of the revelation settling upon him. The intricacies of the plot, the depth of the deception, the cold calculation behind it all, left him reeling. He had been so close to convicting an innocent man, a mistake that could have had devastating consequences. He studied the faces of the Stow family, imagining the roles they played in this intricate web of deception. The carefully constructed facade of grief, the deceptive displays of concern, the subtle manipulations – it was a masterclass in deceit.

Giallo detailed the manner in which the two conspirators had played upon Marlow's own biases and assumptions, skillfully diverting his attention from the true perpetrators while simultaneously building a compelling case against Timothy. He pointed out how the timing of Lucy Stow's death, the positioning of the evidence, and the manipulation of witnesses, had all contributed to creating a convincing narrative of Timothy's guilt. The depth of their scheme was stunning, the sheer audacity of their plan leaving him breathless.

Marlow ran a hand through his already disheveled hair, his gaze fixed on the documents spread across his desk. The weight of his potential error, the near miscarriage of justice, pressed down on him. "And the motive?" he asked, his voice barely a whisper.

Giallo, without missing a beat, explained the meticulous financial planning behind the murder, detailing how Charles and Emily stood to gain immense wealth from Lucy Stow's death. He laid out the intricate financial machinations, the manipulation of wills and trusts, and the subtle legal loopholes they intended to exploit. It wasn't simply a matter of greed; it was a complex, meticulously planned operation designed to secure their financial future at the expense of others.

The enormity of the conspiracy was overwhelming, the audacity of the plan staggering. Marlow found himself struggling to reconcile the image of the seemingly respectable Charles Stow with the cold-blooded manipulator revealed by Giallo's investigation. The case, once seemingly straightforward, had transformed into a labyrinth of deceit, a testament to human ambition and the lengths people would go to achieve their desires. The weight of his responsibility, the near-miss of a terrible injustice, settled heavily upon him.

The revelation left him feeling stunned, shaken by the realization of how easily a carefully constructed illusion could mask the darkest of intentions. The weight of his near-miss was a heavy burden, a grim reminder of the shadows that lurked beneath the surface of even the most seemingly respectable lives. The quiet ticking of the clock seemed to mock his earlier confidence, each tick a stark reminder of the fragility of justice and the potential for even the most experienced investigators to be misled. The confrontation left Marlow deeply unsettled, challenging his perceptions of justice and highlighting the deceptive nature of appearances.

CHAPTER 15
Gathering the Pieces

The scent of woodsmoke and damp earth clung to Giallo as he left Marlow's office, the weight of the revelation settling heavily on his shoulders. The Inspector's stunned silence had spoken volumes, a testament to the audacity of Charles and Emily's scheme. He had initially suspected a straightforward case of murder for inheritance, but the truth, once uncovered, was far more intricate, a chilling masterpiece of deception woven from carefully placed clues and manufactured alibis.

The first piece of the puzzle, he recalled, had been the seemingly insignificant detail of the broken window latch in Timothy's room. Initially dismissed as accidental, Giallo had recognized the precise manner in which it was broken – a subtle sign of forced entry, not accidental damage. It was a carefully staged scene, designed to implicate Timothy further. He'd even had a duplicate key made, to ensure that the seemingly forced entry could happen unnoticed and seamlessly.

Then there was the strychnine. While the initial analysis pointed towards a straightforward poisoning, Giallo had noted the minute traces of a less common, but equally potent, variant of the poison found in a seldom-used, antique apothecary's cabinet in the distant west wing. Its presence suggested a deliberate choice, a calculated move to throw off suspicion. The fact that Lucy Stow herself possessed the knowledge, that only experts would understand, to utilize this specific variant was further evidence of Charles and Emily's careful planning and cunning sophistication. The poison wasn't just a random choice; it was a deliberate one. It was intended to obfuscate the evidence and the killer's true identity.

The letter, discovered tucked away in a forgotten drawer of Lucy Stow's writing desk, was the linchpin. Scrawled in a hurried hand, it revealed Charles' desperation, his insatiable greed for Sheldon Hall and the vast fortune it represented.

He'd detailed his plan in excruciating detail: framing Timothy, manipulating evidence, and ensuring Emily's role remained hidden behind a veil of plausible deniability. The letter was a confession disguised as a frantic plea for help, revealing his plan's intricate detail and the lengths he was willing to go to.

Giallo retraced his steps, mentally revisiting each scene, each conversation. The inconsistencies, previously overlooked, now leaped out at him. Timothy's supposed lack of alibi, for example, had been too convenient, too perfectly crafted to be accidental. It was a planned absence, a deliberate maneuver designed to make him appear guilty. The so-called "witnesses" who had "seen" Timothy near the scene of the crime were merely accomplices, their testimony carefully rehearsed and believable, only to an untrained eye.

The details in their accounts lacked depth, only hitting the major points that pointed directly to Timothy, conveniently ignoring other pertinent details that could have disproven their accounts. The meticulous planning extended to Emily's role. While she hadn't directly participated in the murder, she had been the architect of the deception, using her charm and social standing to create an atmosphere of suspicion around Timothy, subtly influencing the investigation's course. Her impeccable social standing and charming demeanor allowed her to act as an unwitting accomplice, allowing her to feed information and influence others without causing any suspicion. It was a brilliant manipulation, a subtle dance of deceit, perfectly choreographed to conceal her involvement.

Giallo realised the depth of their deception extended beyond the immediate events surrounding Lucy Stow's death. The pair had systematically manipulated their surroundings and relationships, creating a web of interconnected lies that stretched far beyond the walls of Sheldon Hall. They'd skillfully planted evidence, subtly manipulated witnesses, and played upon the pre-existing tensions within the family to create the perfect storm of circumstantial evidence. Their actions showcased not just a desire for wealth, but a terrifying mastery of manipulation and control. They were sophisticated criminals who carefully calculated their every move, using the intricate social dynamics of the era to their advantage, leveraging class distinctions and social pressures to create plausible deniability.

The audacity of their plan was breathtaking. They had taken advantage of the legal system, exploiting the principle of double jeopardy to ensure Timothy's freedom and their own impunity. It was a gamble, a high-stakes game played with lives and reputations, but one they had almost won. Charles and Emily's plan wasn't just about the inheritance; it was about power and control, a display of their superior intellect and cunning. It was a statement of their ability to bend the law, social norms, and human emotions to their will.

Giallo considered the implications. The case wasn't merely about a wealthy widow murdered for her inheritance; it was a chilling exposé on the dark underbelly of ambition, the lengths people would go to achieve their desires, and the chilling ease with which they could manipulate the very systems designed to protect them. It was a study in human nature, revealing the fragility of justice and the subtle ways in which deceit could masquerade as truth.

He reviewed the evidence one last time, piecing together the fragments into a complete picture, ensuring that there was no gap in his analysis. The broken window latch, the rare strychnine, the incriminating letter, the conveniently absent alibi, and Emily's subtle influence – each piece fitted perfectly into the intricate jigsaw puzzle of their carefully constructed lie. There was no room for doubt.

He knew his next step. He wouldn't just present the evidence to Marlow; he would paint a picture, a story so compelling, so undeniable, that it would leave the Inspector and even Charles himself with no choice but to accept the truth. He had to present the case in a manner that highlighted the intricate details of their deception, allowing the truth to reveal itself naturally rather than through forceful presentation. He would meticulously highlight the points of inconsistencies, the subtle shifts in behavior, the carefully chosen words that revealed the truth hidden behind them. His narrative would not only focus on the incriminating details but also weave a story that exposed the true nature of Charles' character, illuminating the motivations behind his actions and the extent of his moral corruption.

As Giallo prepared to confront Charles and Emily, he felt a grim satisfaction. He had unraveled their intricate web of deceit, exposed their carefully constructed illusion, and now, he would bring them to justice. The weight of his responsibility, the near-miss of a terrible injustice, had settled on him heavier this time. He would ensure that the weight of the system would not fall on the innocent, and this time, the clock's ticking would signal the approaching doom of the perpetrators. The game was far from over. The final act was yet to begin. The truth, he knew, was a powerful weapon, capable of shattering the most meticulously crafted lies. And he was ready to unleash it.

CHAPTER 16
Searching for Clues

The late afternoon sun cast long shadows across the manicured lawns of Sheldon Hall, painting the ancient stone in hues of amber and grey. Reeves Giallo, his trench coat pulled tight against the chill autumn air, felt a familiar knot of unease tighten in his stomach. The seemingly idyllic setting belied the dark secret it held, a secret that had claimed the life of Lucy Stow and threatened to ensnare several others in its deadly web. Inspector Marlow, with his impatient pronouncements of Timothy's guilt, had left Giallo with the unsatisfying feeling of a puzzle only half-solved. The evidence, while pointing towards Timothy, Felt…contrived….Too neat….Too convenient. It was the kind of tidiness that screamed of deliberate manipulation.

His investigation had thus far revealed a tangled tapestry of lies, half-truths, and simmering resentments within the Stow family. He had uncovered a clandestine affair between Charles Stow and his cousin, Emily Grace, a secret passion that could easily explain their desperate attempt to frame Timothy. Yet, the motive remained elusive. Why had they risked so much? The inheritance, while substantial, felt insufficient to justify such a calculated and audacious murder. There had to be something more, a deeper, more compelling reason. Giallo began his methodical search anew, focusing on areas he had previously overlooked. He revisited the library, its shelves lined with leather-bound volumes, the air thick with the scent of aged paper and dust. He meticulously examined each book, running his fingers along the spines, searching for any sign of tampering, any hidden compartment, any clue that had escaped his initial scrutiny.

The ornate desk in the corner, with its intricate carvings and secret drawers, held no further surprises. He had already thoroughly examined it.

Next, he moved to the seldom-used west wing of the house, a labyrinth of dusty corridors and forgotten rooms. The air here was colder, heavy with a musty scent, hinting at years of neglect and secrets left undisturbed. He explored each room methodically, his keen eyes scanning every detail, from the chipped paint on the walls to the faded tapestries hanging from the walls. He found nothing in the guest rooms, nor in the servants' quarters, their spartan furnishings a stark contrast to the opulence of the main house.

He found a small, almost forgotten, attic access door tucked away in the darkest corner of the corridor. The door was heavily secured with a rusted lock, and the wood was warped with age, suggesting it had not been opened in many years. With a grunt of exertion, he managed to force the door open, revealing a ladder leading up into the darkness. Dust motes danced in the single beam of his flashlight as he ascended, the air growing increasingly thick with the smell of decay and forgotten things.

The attic space was vast, filled with forgotten furniture shrouded in white sheets, antique trunks bound in leather, and cobwebs thick as shrouds. The air was thick with the smell of mildew and decay. He shone his light across the cluttered space, his eyes scanning each item with a methodical precision. He examined old portraits, their painted eyes staring vacantly into the darkness, seeming to hold unspoken secrets. He moved slowly, cautiously, his footsteps echoing in the cavernous space.

He spent hours combing through the attic's contents, sorting through discarded furniture, dusty boxes, and forgotten family heirlooms. He discovered faded photographs, yellowed letters, and broken toys, each a silent testament to the lives lived within Sheldon Hall.

He was on the verge of giving up, convinced there were no further clues to be found, when his flashlight beam fell upon a small, almost invisible crack in the wall, hidden behind a pile of tattered tapestries.

Using a small, silver letter opener, a memento from his days as a student, he carefully pried the tapestry away. The crack, scarcely larger than a finger, revealed a small, wooden box, carefully hidden behind the wall. His heart pounded in his chest, a thrill of anticipation coursing through him. This was it. He had a feeling. He felt a shiver down his spine, the kind you get before a moment of great revelation. This had to be it.

The small box was locked, secured by a delicate brass clasp. He attempted to force it open, but the lock was surprisingly sturdy, resisting his initial efforts. After several minutes of careful manipulation, the clasp finally yielded, releasing the box's contents. Inside, nestled amongst layers of faded velvet, lay a single letter, sealed with an old wax stamp. The paper was brittle with age, its edges yellowed and frayed, but the handwriting on the envelope was impeccably clear: "To my dearest Lucy, from your devoted Edward."

Giallo carefully unfolded the letter, his eyes scanning the faded script. The handwriting was elegant and precise, the words flowing smoothly across the page. The letter detailed a complex web of financial manipulations and hidden debts, revealing Lucy Stow's secret involvement in a risky investment scheme. Edward, it turned out, was her business partner, a man who was heavily indebted to several powerful figures. Lucy had been on the verge of exposing his fraudulent activities, a fact that could have resulted in his ruin and the ruin of other figures within the local business elite.

The letter explicitly stated that if Lucy ever revealed the truth about Edward's shady dealings, her life would be in grave danger.

This explained the strychnine, the apparent suicide, the carefully orchestrated attempt to frame Timothy. The entire plot was designed to hide Lucy's death as an act of desperation and to protect Edward's secret transactions from ever seeing the light of day.

The letter confirmed Giallo's suspicions. Charles and Emily hadn't been driven by greed alone. They had been pawns in a much larger game, a game orchestrated by a man they didn't even know, a man who had likely paid them handsomely for their silence. But why had they become involved in the first place?

The letter provided a partial explanation, hinting at a long-standing feud between Edward and the Stow family, a feud rooted in decades of bitter resentment and business rivalry. This rivalry stretched back generations, its roots entangled in property disputes and financial maneuvers, a tangled conflict that had seemingly been settled decades ago, only to resurface with Lucy's unexpected death. The letter revealed that Edward's debts were so massive that revealing the truth could have brought not only Edward down but other wealthy figures in the town.

The implications were staggering. The carefully orchestrated narrative of a simple inheritance dispute was shattered, revealing a web of intrigue and deceit that extended far beyond the walls of Sheldon Hall. He had unraveled the true motive, a motive far more sinister and complex than he could have ever imagined. The seemingly simple murder was in fact a complex play on business transactions and political motivations of an otherwise unremarkable family from an ordinary town. He knew now that justice would be served, but not in the way Inspector Marlow anticipated. This case was far from over.

CHAPTER 17
A Hidden Compartment

The weight of the revelation pressed down on Giallo. He'd pieced together the fragments of a meticulously crafted lie, a narrative woven with such skill it had almost fooled him. Charles and Emily, lovers conspiring to inherit Sheldon Hall, had manipulated events with chilling precision. But the motive, while audacious, remained somewhat... incomplete. There were missing pieces, gaps in the carefully constructed puzzle. He needed more. He needed proof.

He returned to Lucy Stow's study, the air thick with the lingering scent of old books and dust. The room, previously meticulously examined, now felt different, charged with a newfound urgency. He ran a hand along the richly carved mahogany desk, tracing the grain with a thoughtful frown. The room had yielded little before, only the carefully placed letters and documents that had served as the foundation of the false narrative. But something felt...off. There was a sense of concealment, a deliberate effort to hide something more.

His eyes fell upon the ornate writing desk, a piece of furniture that seemed to exude an air of quiet authority. He'd examined it thoroughly, but perhaps not thoroughly enough. He ran his fingers along its surface again, searching for any irregularities, any hint of a hidden compartment. The wood was smooth, polished to a high sheen, yet... There, near the left-hand drawer, he felt a subtle indentation, almost imperceptible to the touch. A pressure point?

With a slow, deliberate movement, he pressed the indentation. A soft click echoed in the otherwise silent room, and a section of the desk panel sprang open, revealing a small, concealed compartment. Inside, nestled amongst faded velvet, lay a single, cream-colored envelope. The paper was brittle with age, its edges frayed, but the elegant script on the front suggested a handwriting of some importance.

His heart pounded in his chest as he carefully extracted the letter. The seal was unbroken, hinting at the letter's importance and the careful concealment of its contents. He gently broke the seal, the crackle of the aged paper sending a shiver down his spine. The script within was formal, almost chillingly precise. It was written in Lucy Stow's hand, but the tone was unlike anything he'd encountered in her previous correspondence. It wasn't the sentimental ramblings of a grieving mother, nor the cold businesslike tone of a woman managing her estate. This was… different.

The letter began with a chilling admission: "My dearest Timothy," it read, "I confess a truth I have kept buried for far too long, a truth that threatens not only my family's reputation but also the very fabric of our social standing." Lucy Stow revealed a dark secret, a clandestine affair involving a powerful and influential member of the community, a man whose name was synonymous with respectability and power. This man, Sir Reginald Hawthorne, a prominent figure known for his philanthropy and impeccable character, had a child out of wedlock. Timothy.

The letter went on to explain how Lucy, desperate to shield her son from the scandal and preserve the family's reputation, had orchestrated a complex web of deceit. She had used her influence and connections to secure financial deals and investments that were not always above board. This was her way to build a future for Timothy without tarnishing his image, to ensure his social standing. She had hidden her actions carefully, knowing the consequences if her secret were ever revealed.

However, her actions were not only self-preserving; there was a darker motivation within this protective scheme. She feared that the revelation of her secret would lead to a financial downfall, not only for Timothy but also for Charles, who was heavily entangled in her financial dealings. The complex business ventures, the investments in questionable enterprises, all pointed to a carefully constructed system that propped up a façade of wealth and respectability.

Lucy's death, she wrote, was not an accident. She hinted at an insidious plot, a conspiracy aimed at silencing her before she could reveal the true extent of her network of financial dealings and potentially expose Sir Reginald Hawthorne, a man whose influence extended far beyond the sleepy village of Sheldon. She seemed to suggest that her death was not a simple case of poisoning but a deliberate act, a silencing executed with cold-blooded precision.

The final paragraph was the most chilling. She confessed to having hidden a significant sum of money, funds obtained through her questionable enterprises, somewhere within Sheldon Hall. The letter seemed to suggest that the location was not simply a physical space but a symbol – a metaphor of the hidden truth she'd been hiding all along. This sum was substantial enough to significantly influence the family's future, and could easily cause a fierce battle for control of the estate.

Giallo re-read the letter several times, each reading revealing new layers of intrigue. The meticulously crafted deception, the carefully concealed truth, the intricate network of financial dealings - it was a masterpiece of calculated manipulation. Lucy's death was not a simple act of greed or inheritance dispute, but a consequence of a web of secrets, lies, and illicit transactions. The apparent simplicity of the crime was a masterful illusion designed to hide the far more sinister truth behind her demise.

The implications were profound. Charles and Emily's scheme, while reprehensible, paled in comparison to the vast conspiracy Lucy's letter had unveiled. They had not simply plotted to inherit Sheldon Hall; they had been pawns in a much larger game, a game of power and influence, of social standing and financial control, a game controlled by forces far beyond their grasp.

He looked around the room, the atmosphere now thick with the weight of the revelations. The meticulously crafted facade of the Stow family, the air of respectability that had cloaked their existence, had crumbled before him. The hidden compartment, the meticulously concealed letter, revealed a hidden world, a world of dark secrets, hushed conspiracies, and deadly consequences.

His thoughts raced. The Inspector would have dismissed the letter as another piece of circumstantial evidence, another puzzle piece in the complex game. But Giallo saw beyond the surface; he saw the carefully woven tapestry of deceit, the intricate threads of conspiracy, the deadly consequences of hidden motives. He now knew he had to tread carefully, meticulously weaving together the threads of truth to reveal the full extent of Lucy Stow's legacy and the conspiracy that had ended her life.

The sun dipped below the horizon, casting long, ominous shadows across the room. The once-peaceful study felt oppressive, a silent witness to years of carefully concealed secrets. The letter in his hand felt heavy, weighing down on him, not just with the weight of the paper but with the knowledge of a sinister plot and the weight of a secret that had the potential to destroy more than one family. The game was far from over. The truth, buried beneath layers of deception, was slowly, painstakingly, being unearthed. And Giallo, the unlikely detective, was determined to uncover every single dark detail.

The letter, a silent testament to Lucy Stow's hidden anxieties and fears, was the key to unlocking the true motives behind her death. It was a clue that transcended the simple inheritance dispute, revealing a far more complex and dangerous game of power, influence, and meticulously hidden secrets. The ramifications of this revelation were staggering, reaching beyond Sheldon Hall and the quiet town where it stood, touching the highest echelons of society. Sir Reginald Hawthorne, the pillar of the community, the epitome of respectability, was now inextricably linked to this web of deceit, his reputation on the line.

Giallo's mind raced, piecing together the fragments of information. The letter, the hidden compartment, the meticulously crafted alibi of Timothy, all suddenly fit into place, revealing a sinister orchestration far grander than he had initially imagined. The meticulously crafted plan was designed to mislead, to obscure the truth behind a web of carefully woven lies. But now, with the letter in his hands, the truth was beginning to surface.

The carefully constructed illusion of a simple inheritance dispute had shattered, revealing the darker, more insidious realities that lay beneath. He knew now that his investigation had reached a critical point. The case was no longer about an inheritance dispute; it was about uncovering a conspiracy that threatened to shake the very foundations of the social order. The path ahead was fraught with danger, leading him through a maze of lies and deceit, into a world where respectability was a mask concealing far darker realities.

As he left the study, the weight of the revelation hung heavy in the air, leaving him with a profound sense of foreboding. The path to justice would be far more complex than he had ever imagined. The seemingly straightforward murder of Lucy Stow had opened a Pandora's box, unleashing a torrent of secrets that would threaten to engulf not only Sheldon Hall but the entire town. The investigation, he realized, was far from over; in fact, it had only just begun. The unraveling of the truth, he knew, would be a dangerous and complex task, one that would require all his skill, cunning, and courage. The hidden compartment had yielded its secrets, but the true depth of the conspiracy was still buried deep, waiting to be unearthed.

CHAPTER 18
The Contents of the Letter

The brittle parchment crackled under Giallo's careful touch. The faded ink, barely clinging to the paper, spoke of a clandestine affair, of whispered promises and desperate calculations. The letter, tucked away in the hidden compartment of Lucy Stow's writing desk, was a confession, a damning testament to Charles and Emily's elaborate deception.

It began simply enough, a seemingly innocuous greeting penned in Emily's elegant script. "My dearest Charles," it read, the words a stark contrast to the chilling details that followed. Giallo traced the elegant flourishes, feeling a sudden chill despite the warmth of the study. He could almost hear their voices, their hushed conversations echoing across the years.

The letter then delved into the mechanics of their plot, a chillingly detailed account of their calculated steps. It wasn't just a simple inheritance scheme; it was a meticulously crafted masterpiece of manipulation, each move carefully planned to deflect suspicion onto Timothy. Emily described how she'd subtly poisoned Lucy's sherry, using a nearly undetectable amount of strychnine obtained through a seemingly innocuous connection – a local apothecary with a penchant for discretion and a healthy disregard for the law. The timing, she noted with chilling precision, was critical, coinciding with Timothy's absence from the house, a detail she'd cleverly arranged.

"The alibi," Emily's script continued, "was the most crucial element. We needed to make sure Timothy couldn't be near Sheldon Hall at the time of the poisoning. My subtle suggestion of a late-night rendezvous with his… friend … in the village, a suggestion he readily accepted, solidified his absence.

The fabricated argument, witnessed by the ever-so-observant Mrs. Periwinkle, sealed it. Perfection, wouldn't you agree?"

The final phrase, dripping with a chilling nonchalance, sent a shiver down Giallo's spine.

The letter revealed a disturbing intimacy between Charles and Emily, an unspoken understanding that transcended their shared ambition. Their love, it seemed, was as calculated as their crime. Their feelings were less about passion and more about a shared hunger for wealth and power, a twisted alliance forged in the crucible of greed. The letter detailed their shared financial struggles, the mounting debts that had driven them to such desperate measures. Sheldon Hall, with its vast estates and substantial assets, wasn't just a prize; it was their salvation.

"Remember our conversation at the races, darling?" Emily wrote. "How you fretted about the mounting debts, the looming threat of creditors. Sheldon Hall... it's our escape, our redemption. The life we deserve."

Giallo paused, letting the weight of those words sink in. Their love was a transactional one, bound by their shared ambition, their mutual desperation. It was a love born not from affection, but from a cold, calculated desire for financial security. It was a testament to the corrosive power of greed, twisting even the most profound human emotions into tools of manipulation.

The letter then detailed the subtle ways they'd planted the evidence, the seemingly insignificant details designed to incriminate Timothy. A carelessly placed handkerchief bearing Timothy's monogram near Lucy's body; a half-written note hinting at a bitter argument between mother and son. Every detail, meticulously orchestrated, pointed towards Timothy's guilt.

"The Inspector is quite easily swayed," Emily wrote, her words tinged with a hint of arrogance. "He'll jump at the opportunity to pin this on Timothy; his impulsive nature will do the rest."

The letter confirmed Giallo's suspicions: Inspector Marlow's rush to judgement wasn't simply incompetence; it was a carefully orchestrated result of Charles and Emily's machinations.

As Giallo continued to read, the letter detailed their plan to exploit the legal loopholes, utilizing the law of double jeopardy to their advantage. They were so confident in their deception that they felt safe, untouchable. They hadn't anticipated Giallo's keen eye for detail, his ability to see beyond the surface, to uncover the intricate web of lies they'd so carefully spun.

But amidst the chilling detail of their plot, Giallo discovered a subtler narrative, a counterpoint to their greed-fueled ambition. Interwoven with the cold, calculated details of their scheme were glimpses of a more vulnerable Emily, a woman wrestling with the moral implications of her actions.

There were fleeting moments of doubt, hesitant strokes of the pen, as if she was grappling with the enormity of what they were doing.

One passage caught Giallo's attention: "Charles, my darling, sometimes, in the quiet of the night, I wonder if we've gone too far. The guilt… it gnaws at me. But the thought of the life we could have, of escaping this crushing debt… it keeps me going. Forgive me, but I can't turn back now."

This confession, hidden amongst the meticulously crafted lies, painted a more nuanced picture of Emily. She wasn't simply a cold-hearted accomplice; she was a woman trapped in a web of her own making, caught between her love for Charles and the weight of her conscience.

It wasn't merely ambition; it was a desperate attempt to secure a future, a future free from the crushing weight of poverty and despair. It was a tragic tale, a cautionary narrative of how desperation can corrupt even the purest intentions.

The letter ended abruptly, the final sentence unfinished:

"We must…" The rest was lost, swallowed by the ravages of time and decay. The unfinished sentence hung in the air, a poignant reminder of the unresolved conflicts, the unspoken doubts that lurked beneath the surface of their meticulously planned scheme.

Giallo closed the letter, the weight of its revelation pressing down on him. He had uncovered the truth, the intricate tapestry of deceit woven by Charles and Emily. But the truth, he realized, was more complex than he had initially imagined. It wasn't simply a tale of greed and ambition; it was a story of love, desperation, and the devastating consequences of choices made under duress.

The letter had revealed not just the perpetrators of Lucy Stow's murder but also a tragic reflection of the times, a stark commentary on the desperation that gripped society during the war years, driving people to unthinkable acts in the pursuit of survival and a better future.

The investigation, he knew, was far from over. The implications of this letter reached far beyond the confines of Sheldon Hall; it touched upon the very fabric of society, exposing the fragility of morality in the face of extreme circumstances. The unraveling of this truth would be a far more treacherous path than he'd originally anticipated, one that demanded not only his intellect but his profound understanding of human nature, its capacity for both great evil and unexpected compassion.

CHAPTER 19
The Weight of Revelation

The implications of the letter were far-reaching, a seismic shift in the narrative that left Giallo reeling. He reread the faded script, each word a dagger piercing the carefully constructed facade of the case. Charles Stow, the seemingly grieving friend, the inheritor unjustly accused, was revealed to be the architect of Lucy Stow's demise, his love for Emily Grace the driving force behind his calculated treachery. The letter detailed their plan, a meticulously crafted scheme to eliminate Lucy and secure the Sheldon Hall estate for themselves. It spoke of forged documents, subtly manipulated alibis, and the insidious planting of false evidence to implicate Timothy, Lucy's son, diverting suspicion away from the true culprits.

The elegant script, betraying a practiced hand, detailed the meticulous planning. Each step, each carefully placed clue, was laid out with chilling precision. It was a masterpiece of deception, a testament to their cunning, and a chilling reflection of their ruthlessness. The war, with its pervasive atmosphere of uncertainty and loss, had clearly warped their perceptions, fueling their desperate ambition. Their actions weren't simply borne out of greed, but desperation, a frantic grasp for a future seemingly snatched away by the brutal realities of conflict. The letter served as a chilling chronicle of their descent into darkness, a tale whispered in the shadows of a world consumed by war.

The weight of this revelation pressed upon Giallo. He had expected a simple case of inheritance disputes and cunning manipulation; instead, he'd unearthed a conspiracy rooted in a far deeper, more disturbing desperation. The letter exposed not only a murder but also a profound moral failing, a commentary on the corrosive effects of war and the fragility of human morality when pushed to its limits. This wasn't just a crime; it was a reflection of a society fractured by conflict, a society where even the most trusted relationships could crumble under the weight of desperate circumstances.

He looked up from the letter, his gaze settling on the portrait of Lucy Stow, her serene face a stark contrast to the turmoil brewing within the walls of Sheldon Hall. The seemingly idyllic estate now felt suffocating, heavy with the weight of secrets and betrayals. He pondered the implications for Inspector Marlow, a man driven by duty and a rigid adherence to procedure. Marlow, convinced of

Timothy's guilt, would find it difficult, perhaps impossible, to accept such a radical reversal of fortune. The evidence, meticulously planted by Charles and Emily, had been so convincing, so damning, that it would require a Herculean effort to persuade him of its fraudulent nature. The thought of confronting Marlow filled Giallo with a mixture of dread and anticipation. He knew the inspector wouldn't easily accept his findings, particularly given his initial certainty of Timothy's culpability. The reputation of Scotland Yard, and indeed, his own reputation, was at stake. He would have to present the evidence with meticulous care, leaving no room for doubt, no loophole for Marlow to cling to his initial assumptions. The weight of proving his findings was immense, a responsibility that rested heavily upon his shoulders. He had to tread carefully, navigating the precarious terrain of officialdom and established procedures.

One misstep, one misplaced word, could derail the entire investigation and allow the true culprits to escape justice. The letter, however, provided Giallo with more than just a confession; it was a roadmap, a meticulously detailed account of their actions. It was a guide that illuminated their every move, from the initial planning stages to the final, fatal act.

The letter revealed the acquisition of the strychnine, a seemingly insignificant detail that had gone unnoticed during the initial investigation. It detailed the precise method of administration, highlighting the knowledge and expertise needed to carry out such a sophisticated plan. Furthermore, the letter confirmed their involvement in the forging of key documents, a detail that would prove crucial in their prosecution.

Giallo's mind raced, piecing together the puzzle, each detail interlocking with the others, forming a comprehensive and irrefutable picture of their guilt. The letter was not merely a confession; it was a masterclass in criminal procedure, a testament to their planning and sophistication. He realized that the letter itself was a crucial piece of evidence, a smoking gun that could not be ignored. It was a detailed confession, a roadmap of their crime, and a damning testament to their culpability.

He considered the implications for Emily Grace. While her involvement was undeniable, her motive remained more ambiguous. The letter hinted at a desperate love, a desperate attempt to secure a future amidst the turmoil of war. Was it a love born of genuine affection or a cynical calculation? Was she a willing accomplice or a manipulated pawn in Charles' grand scheme? These questions gnawed at Giallo, forcing him to confront the complexity of human motivation and the tangled web of emotions that drive individuals to commit unspeakable acts. The letter offered glimpses into her state of mind, her desperation, her fear, and her complicity. But it did not fully explain the depth of her involvement, leaving Giallo to grapple with the nuanced nature of her culpability. Was she merely a pawn, or was she as deeply implicated as Charles?

The weight of the revelation extended beyond Charles and Emily. Timothy, initially the prime suspect, now stood exonerated, his relief overshadowed by the shock of discovering the treachery of those he considered friends.

The letter revealed a betrayal far deeper than he could have ever imagined, a deception that had almost cost him his freedom, his reputation, and possibly his life. His initial suspicious behavior, so easily misinterpreted, now held a new meaning, a new context. He had been framed, manipulated, and used as a pawn in a larger, more sinister game. The understanding of this betrayal, the sheer audacity of the scheme, would undoubtedly leave a lasting impact on his life, changing his perception of trust and friendship forever.

The letter also forced Giallo to reassess his own role in the investigation. His initial suspicions, while initially directed at Timothy, had been subtly guided, manipulated by the subtle clues planted by Charles and Emily. He had been a skilled detective, yet he had been outmaneuvered, outwitted by the cunning minds of the perpetrators. He had been played, as much as Timothy had been, a humbling realization that only underscored the complexity of human nature and the endless possibilities of deception.

This realization wasn't just a setback, however; it served as a valuable learning experience, sharpening his understanding of criminal psychology and the intricate dance of detection and deception. The discovery of the letter had shattered the initial narrative, sending Giallo on a new path of investigation. The investigation was no longer a simple matter of identifying the murderer; it was a journey into the heart of darkness, a descent into a world of betrayal, manipulation, and desperate ambition. He knew he had to unravel the full extent of Charles and Emily's scheme, ensuring that justice would prevail. The letter was a crucial piece of the puzzle, but it was only a piece.

There were undoubtedly further layers to uncover, more secrets to unearth, and more truths to reveal. The weight of revelation, far from bringing closure, had only deepened the mystery, opening up new avenues of inquiry.

Giallo knew this was just the beginning of a far more intricate and treacherous path, a path that demanded both his skills and his resolve. The investigation, now enriched by the revelation of the letter, had transformed from a simple murder case to a complex exploration of the human psyche, a poignant commentary on the desperation of a world at war. The journey ahead would be perilous, fraught with dangers both foreseen and unforeseen, but Giallo, armed with the truth revealed by the letter, was ready to confront the challenges that lay ahead. The truth, he knew, was far from simple and the quest for justice would be anything but easy.

CHAPTER 20
Confrontation and Revelation

The rain lashed against the windows of Sheldon Hall, mirroring the tempest brewing within Giallo. He stood before Charles Stow and Emily Grace, the flickering firelight casting long, dancing shadows that seemed to mock the stillness of their defiance. The letter, clutched in his hand, felt heavy, a tangible weight of their deceit. He had carefully chosen this moment, the late evening hours cloaked in the oppressive atmosphere of the storm, to confront them. The air crackled with unspoken accusations, the silence broken only by the rhythmic drumming of the rain.

"I believe you have some explaining to do," Giallo began, his voice calm but firm, a stark contrast to the turmoil within him. He laid the letter on the antique table between them, its faded ink a stark testament to their carefully constructed lies. Charles' face, usually composed, betrayed a flicker of panic, quickly masked by a forced composure. Emily, her usual ethereal beauty marred by a strained pallor, shifted uneasily, her eyes darting nervously around the room.

Charles opened his mouth to speak, but Giallo held up a hand, silencing him.

"Let's dispense with the charade, shall we? The letter leaves little to the imagination. Your meticulous plan, the forged documents, the subtle manipulation of Timothy's alibi – it's all laid bare."

He paused, letting the weight of his words sink in. The silence that followed was heavy, thick with the unspoken confessions hanging in the air.

Emily finally spoke, her voice a fragile whisper.

"How...how did you find it?" Her gaze was pleading, desperate for a shred of hope in the face of their exposed treachery.

Giallo met her gaze, his expression unyielding.

"Let's just say, some secrets are harder to keep than others. The desperation in your actions, your clumsy attempts to cover your tracks, they all led me to the truth. The letter was the final piece, the key that unlocked your carefully constructed puzzle."

He gestured towards the letter again.

"It speaks volumes about your ambition, your love, and the lengths you were willing to go to secure Sheldon Hall."

Charles, regaining some of his composure, scoffed.

"You've built a case on circumstantial evidence. A letter, a mere piece of paper, can hardly condemn us."

His voice, though confident, held a tremor of uncertainty. The bravado was a thin veneer, barely concealing the fear gnawing at him.

"Circumstantial, perhaps," Giallo conceded, "but the circumstances are overwhelmingly incriminating. The letter details not just the plan but the meticulous execution. The forged documents, the planting of the strychnine, the manipulation of Timothy – it's a masterclass in deception, if not a masterclass in morality. Your plan was almost flawless, but you overlooked one crucial element: human nature. Your desperation, your eagerness to cover your tracks, betrayed you."

He leaned forward, his voice dropping to a near whisper.

"You underestimated the power of observation, Charles. You underestimated my determination. You underestimated the justice system itself."

Emily, her composure finally shattering, began to weep. The carefully crafted mask of innocence crumbled, revealing the raw emotion beneath.

Charles, however, remained outwardly stoic, though the tightening of his jaw betrayed his inner turmoil.
Giallo continued, his voice unwavering.

"You believed the law of double jeopardy would shield you. You thought that by framing Timothy, you could escape unscathed. But you failed to consider the possibility that the evidence, cleverly planted though it was, could be traced back to you. You believed in your cleverness, but you underestimated the tenacity of a determined investigator."

He recounted the intricacies of their plan, meticulously detailing how they had manipulated the events leading up to Lucy Stow's death. He spoke of the forged documents, the subtle changes they had made to the will, the deliberate placement of the strychnine vial, the carefully orchestrated alibis. Each detail was a blow, each revelation a further stripping away of their carefully constructed facade.

The room was silent save for Emily's quiet sobs. Charles, his face pale and drawn, stared into the fire, his eyes reflecting the flames flickering dance. The weight of his actions, the gravity of his deception, was finally beginning to dawn on him. He had played a dangerous game, and he had lost.

Giallo described how he'd discovered the letter, hidden within a secret compartment of Emily's writing desk, a compartment he only discovered through astute observation of an almost imperceptible scratch on the wood. He spoke of the painstaking process of deciphering the faded script, of piecing together the fragments of their plan, of corroborating the details with other evidence found throughout the house.

The process of uncovering their scheme, Giallo explained, wasn't merely a matter of finding the letter. It involved painstaking forensic analysis of the strychnine vial, which revealed a trace of a unique perfume only Emily wore;

examination of the forged documents, which revealed inconsistencies in the ink and paper; and careful study of the movements of both Charles and Emily on the night of the murder, meticulously piecing together their alibis and demonstrating their conflicting accounts.

He detailed the pressure Charles had put on the servants to create false narratives. He explained how the subtle changes to the will, designed to make it seem legitimate on the surface, were ultimately the very changes that provided the evidence he needed to prove their deception.

He explained the financial records, detailing Charles' mounting debts and the significant financial gain he would receive from Lucy Stow's death.

The storm outside raged, a furious symphony of wind and rain. Inside, the silence was thick with the weight of their guilt. The flickering firelight danced on their faces, highlighting the stark contrast between their outward composure and the turmoil within.

"You thought you were clever," Giallo concluded, his voice low but resolute. "You thought you could manipulate fate, manipulate justice. But you underestimated the power of truth. The truth, like the storm raging outside, will always find a way to break through."

Charles, finally breaking his silence, looked at Giallo, his eyes filled with a mixture of regret and defeat.

"It was… it was for Emily," he said, his voice barely a whisper. "I loved her. I would do anything for her."

Emily, her sobs subsiding, looked at Charles, her eyes filled with a mixture of love and despair.

"He did it for me," she whispered. "I never wanted to hurt anyone…"

Giallo remained silent, his gaze unwavering. He had exposed their crimes, but the complexities of their motivations remained. The war had left its mark on them, creating a landscape of desperation and deceit.

Their love, twisted and corrupted by ambition, had led them down a path of destruction. Justice would be served, but the underlying darkness, the human cost of their actions, would linger long after the case was closed. The rain outside continued its relentless assault, a fitting backdrop to the shattered remnants of their carefully constructed world. The storm had passed, revealing the wreckage of their lives, a stark testament to the destructive power of greed and the seductive allure of forbidden love. The confrontation was over, but the echoes of their deception would resonate for years to come.

CHAPTER 21
The Arrest

The rain hammered against the leaded windows of Sheldon Hall, mirroring the tempest brewing inside Inspector Marlow's usually placid demeanor. He stood rigidly, his polished boots gleaming dully under the harsh gaslight, as Reeves Giallo calmly surveyed the scene. Charles Stow, his face ashen, his usually impeccable attire rumpled, stood handcuffed in the center of the grand hall, his shoulders slumped in defeat. Beside him, Emily Grace, her elegant composure shattered, stared blankly ahead, her usually vibrant eyes clouded with a mixture of shock and despair.

The arrest hadn't been a dramatic showdown, no desperate struggle or last-ditch attempt at escape. Instead, it had been a quiet, almost anticlimactic surrender. Giallo, having meticulously laid out his case—a tapestry woven from seemingly insignificant details, overlooked inconsistencies, and the damning evidence of the hidden letter—had simply presented Charles and Emily with the inescapable truth.

They had crumbled under the weight of their own deceit. The carefully constructed facade of innocence had shattered, leaving behind only the stark reality of their crime.

Marlow, initially resistant to Giallo's unconventional methods, watched with a mixture of grudging admiration and professional pique. He'd been so sure of Timothy Stow's guilt, blinded by the superficial evidence and the pressure to quickly solve the case. Giallo's meticulous investigation, his ability to see beyond the obvious, had exposed the depths of Charles and Emily's depravity, a testament to his exceptional deductive skills.

The inspector's initial arrogance had been replaced by a quiet respect, tinged with the bitter taste of his own failure to perceive the truth.

The arrest itself was a study in contrasts. The grandeur of Sheldon Hall, a testament to generations of Stow wealth, was starkly juxtaposed with the stark reality of Charles and Emily's predicament. The polished mahogany furniture, the intricate tapestries, the very air heavy with the scent of old money and privilege, seemed to mock their downfall. The contrast highlighted the hollowness of their ambition, their insatiable greed. Their carefully constructed world, built on lies and manipulation, had come crashing down around them, leaving them exposed in their vulnerability.

Constables, their faces impassive beneath their helmets, efficiently secured Charles and Emily, their movements precise and professional. There was no fanfare, no triumphant declaration. The silence in the hall was punctuated only by the rhythmic drumming of the rain and the occasional creak of the ancient floorboards. Even the crackling fire in the vast hearth seemed to have dimmed, as if reflecting the extinguishing of their hopes and aspirations.

The weight of their actions, the consequences of their choices, hung heavy in the air, a palpable presence felt by all present.

The scene was a stark reminder of the fragility of power and the inescapable consequences of deception. The carefully planned web of lies, spun with such meticulous care, had ultimately ensnared its architects. Their elaborate scheme, designed to secure their inheritance and their future, had instead led them to their arrest, their reputations tarnished irrevocably. The very opulence that had fueled their ambition now served as a stark backdrop to their defeat, a symbol of their shattered dreams.

The ensuing interrogation was equally devoid of drama. Charles, stripped of his arrogance, confessed readily, the weight of his guilt crushing him. He spoke of his desperate need for money, his burning desire to restore the Stow family fortune, a fortune he believed rightfully belonged to him. He spoke of Emily, his love for her, a love that had blinded him to the ethical implications of their actions. He had hoped to secure a future for himself and Emily, a life of luxury and comfort, a future he felt justified in claiming, regardless of the means.

Emily, initially defiant, eventually echoed Charles' confession. Her statements confirmed the intricate details of their plan, the meticulous way they had manipulated evidence, planted false clues, and orchestrated Timothy's near downfall. She admitted her part in the scheme, a mixture of ambition and love blinding her to the moral bankruptcy of their actions. She had believed in the righteousness of their cause, a twisted logic born of desperation and love for Charles.

With the confessions secured, the truth was laid bare, a stark and unsettling revelation. Timothy Stow, initially the prime suspect, was released from suspicion. The relief on his face was palpable, a stark contrast to the despair etched onto Charles and Emily's features. The weight of false accusations, the fear of imprisonment, the humiliation of being wrongly suspected, all lifted from his shoulders. He was free, exonerated, yet the ordeal had left an indelible mark on him, a scar on his soul.
The aftermath of the arrests was a whirlwind of activity.

Legal proceedings commenced, the wheels of justice slowly turning. The media, always eager for a sensational story, descended upon Sheldon Hall, their cameras flashing, their microphones capturing every hushed conversation, every whispered rumour. The family name, once synonymous with wealth and respectability, was now sullied, tainted by scandal and deceit.

The veneer of privilege had been peeled away, revealing the ugly truth beneath. Inspector Marlow, though initially disappointed by his failure to solve the case correctly, acknowledged Giallo's brilliance, a grudging admission extracted from his stiff upper lip. The case had served as a painful lesson, reminding him of the limitations of conventional methods and the importance of open-mindedness. He realized the need to question his assumptions and the need to thoroughly investigate each potential avenue of truth. His experience had broadened his approach to investigation, emphasizing observation, critical thinking, and the understanding of human nature. Sheldon Hall itself, the stage for this tragic drama, remained.

But the atmosphere had changed, its heavy air of gloom replaced by a tentative sense of hope and a palpable relief. The shadows of deceit had finally been lifted, leaving behind a fragile dawn of justice. The future of the estate, its inhabitants, their lives, lay uncertain but with the weight of falsehood finally gone, there was a possibility of healing, a path towards a new future. The house, a silent witness to countless secrets, stood resolute, ready for the next chapter of its history, a history that would bear the imprint of this dramatic revelation. The cost of deception, however, was high, leaving lasting scars on all those involved, leaving them to rebuild their lives from the ashes of broken trust and shattered illusions. The tale of Lucy Stow's death served as a cautionary parable of greed, ambition, and the inescapable consequences of betraying trust, a warning etched in the very stones of Sheldon Hall itself.

CHAPTER 22
Timothy's Exoneration

The air in the courtroom crackled with a tension thicker than the fog rolling in from the North Sea. Timothy Stow, his face gaunt and drawn, sat rigidly, his eyes fixed on Inspector Marlow, who stood before the judge, his usual impassive expression momentarily fractured by a flicker of something akin to doubt. Reeves Giallo, his presence as quiet and observant as ever, stood beside him, a silent sentinel against the storm of accusations that had engulfed Timothy for weeks.

The revelation had been explosive, a carefully constructed house of cards collapsing under the weight of Giallo's meticulous investigation. The letter, penned by Charles Stow himself, detailing the intricate plot to frame Timothy, was the final, damning piece of evidence. It painted a picture of cold calculation and ruthless ambition, exposing the lengths to which Charles and Emily Grace would go to secure Sheldon Hall and its considerable fortune. The forged alibi, the subtly planted clues, the manipulation of witnesses – all meticulously planned and flawlessly executed, until Giallo's relentless pursuit of truth unraveled the entire charade.

The judge, a man known for his unwavering fairness, addressed the court with a solemnity that left no room for misinterpretation. He spoke of the blatant disregard for justice, the perversion of the legal process, and the devastating impact of the false accusations on Timothy Stow. He meticulously dissected Giallo's evidence, highlighting the inconsistencies in the initial investigation and the compelling nature of the newly discovered letter. The weight of the evidence, irrefutable and devastating, hung heavy in the air.

The prosecution, initially confident in their case, were now reduced to speechless onlookers, their carefully crafted narrative shattered into a million pieces.

The verdict, when it came, was a resounding acquittal. The words "Not Guilty" echoed through the silent courtroom, reverberating in Timothy's ears, a balm to the wounds inflicted by weeks of unjust imprisonment and suspicion. He looked at his lawyer, Mr. Finch, a man who had staunchly defended him despite the overwhelming evidence presented initially. Mr. Finch, a veteran of countless court battles, had a rare look of genuine relief on his face. He clapped Timothy on the shoulder, a silent affirmation of their shared victory.

The release from custody was not simply a legal formality; it was a restoration of his dignity, a reclaiming of his life. As he stepped out of the courtroom, the weight of the false accusations seemed to lift, replaced by a cautious optimism, a tentative embrace of a future once stolen from him. The rain, which had relentlessly battered the city throughout the trial, suddenly stopped. A single shaft of sunlight broke through the clouds, illuminating the path ahead, a symbol of hope and justice.

But the exoneration wasn't just about Timothy. It was about the shattering of a carefully cultivated illusion, the exposure of a deceit that had poisoned the lives of many. Charles Stow, his face ashen and his eyes devoid of their usual arrogance, sat alone in his cell, the reality of his actions finally sinking in. The weight of his betrayal, the depth of his deception, was a burden too heavy to bear. His dream of possessing Sheldon Hall, of securing Emily Grace's hand in marriage, had crumbled, leaving behind only the bitter taste of failure and the cold certainty of imprisonment.

Emily Grace, too, faced the consequences of her actions. Her carefully constructed façade of sophistication and charm had been stripped away, revealing the calculating woman beneath. The loss of her social standing, the ruin of her reputation, was a price she would pay for her complicity in Charles' schemes. The weight of her betrayal hung heavy upon her, a constant reminder of the choices she had made. The vibrant woman who had once captivated so many with her beauty and wit was now a shadow of her former self, haunted by the ghosts of her past.

The impact of the trial resonated far beyond the courtroom walls. Sheldon Hall, once a symbol of privilege and opulence, now bore the scars of the deceit that had played out within its walls. The whispers and speculation that swirled around the estate were a constant reminder of the tragedy that had unfolded. The family reputation, once held high, lay shattered, a testament to the corrosive power of greed and ambition. The servants, who had witnessed the unfolding drama, were left to grapple with the shattered trust, forced to confront the reality that those they had served were capable of such profound depravity. The aftermath of the trial brought a strange sense of unease to the residents of the nearby village.

The Stow family had always been a significant part of their community, their influence reaching far beyond the confines of Sheldon Hall. The revelation of their duplicity shattered a sense of security, raising questions about the reliability of appearances and the deceptive nature of wealth. The whispers and murmurs that followed served as a constant reminder that even the most outwardly respectable families could harbor dark secrets.
For Timothy, the journey to reclaim his life was far from over. The scars of false accusation ran deep, leaving a lingering sense of uncertainty.

The ordeal had shaken his faith in humanity, leaving him questioning the nature of trust and loyalty. He found solace in the quiet support of his friends, people who had believed in his innocence even when the evidence seemed insurmountable. He worked tirelessly to rebuild his reputation, to prove his worth, to demonstrate the integrity that had been wrongly called into question.

Reeves Giallo, a man who had seen much in his career, was deeply affected by the case. The depth of Charles and Emily's deception, the meticulous nature of their plot, left him pondering the true nature of human malice. He had exposed the truth, but the experience left him with a lingering sense of unease, a reminder of the fragility of justice and the potential for darkness to reside in even the most unsuspecting hearts. He knew that even with the exoneration, the shadow of the case would remain for many years, a constant reminder of the intricate web of deceit that had woven itself into the lives of the Stow family.

The case of Lucy Stow's murder, while seemingly resolved with Timothy's exoneration, left a lasting mark on the lives of everyone involved. The trial itself, a drawn-out and deeply emotional battle for truth, became a cautionary tale. It served as a chilling testament to the destructive nature of ambition, the poisonous influence of greed, and the devastating consequences of betrayal. It was a reminder that appearances can be deceiving and that even behind the most polished facades, the darkest secrets can lurk. The story of Lucy Stow's death, the trial that followed, and the subsequent exoneration of Timothy Stow became a legend whispered in the halls of Sheldon Hall, a chilling tale of deceit and retribution that echoed through the years.

The shadow of the case lingered long after the court proceedings had concluded, a lasting reminder of the enduring power of truth, the importance of justice, and the enduring consequences of human failings. The future remained uncertain, yet there was a fragile hope, a new beginning forged from the ashes of a carefully orchestrated deception. The house itself, silent witness to the drama, stood resolute, its stones bearing the weight of secrets, a reminder that some truths are revealed only through the meticulous pursuit of justice and the unwavering dedication of those who seek it. The true cost of deception, however, remained, etched not only on the lives of those involved but also within the very fabric of Sheldon Hall itself.

CHAPTER 23
Marlow's Reaction

The courtroom emptied slowly, the hush of disbelief hanging heavy in the air long after the gavel fell. Inspector Marlow remained, his gaze fixed on the spot where Timothy Stow had moments before been released, the weight of the day's events pressing down on him like a physical burden. His shoulders slumped, the crispness of his uniform seeming to wilt under the oppressive atmosphere. He hadn't felt this...unsettled... since the early days of the war, the constant barrage of uncertainty and the chilling realization that even the most solid plans could crumble under the weight of unforeseen circumstances. This case had been... different. It hadn't followed the neat lines of his meticulously crafted procedures, the predictable steps that usually led to a satisfying conclusion.

He ran a hand through his already disheveled hair, the gesture betraying a weariness that went beyond the physical fatigue of a long day. His usual methodical approach, a blend of shrewd observation and rigorous procedure, had led him down a blind alley. He had been so certain of Timothy's guilt, the evidence seemingly irrefutable, pointing undeniably towards the young man's avarice and desperation. Yet, Giallo, with his unorthodox methods and almost unsettling intuition, had unravelled the carefully constructed web of deceit, exposing the true culprits with an elegance that bordered on artistry. The contrast between their approaches was stark.

Marlow's method was a product of the rigid system he served, a system that valued order and procedure above all else.
Giallo, on the other hand, operated outside those boundaries, his investigation driven by an almost

instinctual understanding of human nature, a capacity to see beyond the surface, to discern the hidden motives that lay beneath the carefully crafted masks of respectability. Marlow had focused on the tangible – the physical evidence, the alibis, the financial records – while Giallo delved into the intangible – the subtle nuances of human interaction, the unspoken tensions, the concealed desires. And it was Giallo's approach, unconventional and arguably unscientific by Marlow's standards, that had yielded the truth.

A bitter taste lingered in Marlow's mouth; a taste not of defeat, exactly, but of…discomfort. It wasn't simply the failure to apprehend the true perpetrators; it was the realization that his own rigorous adherence to procedure, his reliance on the visible, had nearly led to a grave miscarriage of justice. He had almost condemned an innocent man, a man whose apparent guilt had been so meticulously crafted that even his experienced eyes had failed to see the deception. The thought hung heavy in the air, thick and suffocating. He wasn't used to questioning his methods, his judgment. He prided himself on his efficiency, his unwavering commitment to the facts, but this case had shattered that sense of invincibility. It had forced him to confront the limitations of his own approach, a stark reminder that the truth is not always readily apparent, and sometimes, it takes a different perspective, a different kind of mind, to uncover it.

He walked towards the window, the chill wind whipping his coat around him. The view from Sheldon Hall was breathtaking, the rolling hills and the vast expanse of the sea offering a sense of perspective, a contrast to the claustrophobic intensity of the courtroom. Yet, even the panoramic beauty couldn't fully soothe the turmoil within.

He watched the twilight deepen, painting the sky in hues of orange and purple, a visual representation of the complex emotions swirling inside him. The case had shaken him to his core, challenging his fundamental assumptions about justice, about the very nature of truth.

He considered Giallo's methods. He had always viewed Giallo as an outsider, an eccentric figure operating on the fringes of the established order. But the success of Giallo's unconventional approach forced Marlow to reconsider his own ingrained prejudices. Perhaps, he mused, there was more to the detective's intuitive methods than mere luck or coincidence. Perhaps his ability to understand the human element, the nuances of deception and motive, was a skill as valuable, if not more so, than the rigid adherence to established procedures. The case served as a stark lesson in humility, a humbling reminder that the pursuit of justice is not always a linear path, and that the most elusive truths are often found not in the meticulous examination of facts, but in the insightful interpretation of human behavior.

He thought about Charles Stow and Emily Grace. Their audacious plan, their calculated risk, their almost chilling precision in framing Timothy. It spoke to a level of cunning that Marlow had underestimated, a testament to the depths of human depravity, driven by greed and ambition. He understood the motive, the desire for wealth and power. But it was the cold-blooded calculation, the deliberate manipulation of evidence, that truly disturbed him. It wasn't merely a crime of passion, a spur-of-the-moment act driven by anger or desperation. It was a calculated crime, a carefully orchestrated piece of theatre, played out with an almost chilling precision.

The image of Timothy's gaunt face, etched with the pain of unjust accusation, lingered in Marlow's mind. The young man had faced the weight of the law, the crushing burden of suspicion, with a quiet dignity that had resonated deeply with Marlow. He felt a pang of remorse, a deep sense of regret, at the near miss of a grave injustice. He had been so close to condemning an innocent man, blinded by what he believed to be irrefutable evidence.

The experience, unsettling and profoundly humbling, had opened his eyes to the limitations of his own rigid approach. He understood now the importance of considering all angles, the necessity of going beyond the surface, of delving into the psychological complexities of the human mind.

As darkness descended upon Sheldon Hall, casting long shadows across the grounds, Marlow stood at the window, a silent observer of the night. The wind howled outside, a mournful symphony mirroring the turmoil within him. He realized that his understanding of justice had undergone a profound transformation. It was no longer simply a matter of following established procedures, of adhering to the letter of the law.

It was about seeing the whole picture, understanding the motives, the complexities, the hidden depths of human nature. He had learned a valuable lesson, a painful but ultimately instructive lesson, about the fallibility of his own judgment, the limits of his own perspective, and the subtle, elusive nature of truth. He left Sheldon Hall that night, the weight of the case, and his newfound understanding, settling heavily upon his shoulders.

The case of Lucy Stow's murder would forever remain etched in his memory, not just as a solved case, but as a profound lesson, a testament to the complexities of human nature and the ever-evolving nature of justice. The experience had changed him, sharpening his instincts, broadening his perspective, and reminding him of the vital importance of remaining open to alternative approaches, embracing ambiguity, and accepting that the pursuit of truth is a journey, not a destination, a continuous process of learning, adapting, and evolving. He knew that his methods, his understanding, would never be quite the same again. The shadow of Lucy Stow's murder, and the extraordinary revelation that followed, would forever shape his perception of justice. The weight of the experience was heavy, but he knew, deep down, that it was a weight he had to carry, a weight that would shape him into a better, more insightful detective, more understanding of the subtle intricacies of human deception.

CHAPTER 24
The Aftermath

The heavy oak door of Sheldon Hall creaked shut behind Inspector Marlow, the sound swallowed by the vastness of the estate. The crisp autumn air, carrying the scent of damp earth and decaying leaves, offered little solace to the turmoil within him. The case, officially closed, felt anything but. The revelation of Charles Stow and Emily Grace's elaborate scheme, their callous manipulation of Timothy, had left him reeling. He'd spent his career chasing tangible evidence, concrete facts, but this case had exposed the slippery, elusive nature of truth, hidden beneath layers of deceit and carefully constructed lies. He had arrested criminals before, seen justice served, but this... this felt different. This felt like a betrayal of the very principles he held dear.

Timothy Stow, released from the confines of the local jail, wandered the grounds of Sheldon Hall like a ghost. The weight of the accusations, the public humiliation, the shattered trust, clung to him like a shroud. He'd been exonerated, yes, but the stain remained. His mother's death, the sudden, brutal end to his life as he knew it, left a gaping wound. The initial relief at his release was quickly replaced by a profound sense of loss and disillusionment.

He found himself drawn to the neglected rose garden, a place of vibrant life ironically juxtaposed with the bleakness in his soul. His mother's favorite roses, once meticulously tended, now drooped, their petals withered and falling, mirroring the state of his own spirit. He knelt amongst the wilting blooms, the chill earth seeping into his knees, and let the tears flow, unburdening himself of the silent grief that had choked him for weeks. He had been spared prison, but the sentence of his emotional turmoil felt far more severe.

The future of Sheldon Hall, once a symbol of family and tradition, hung precariously in the balance. The estate, steeped in history and burdened by secrets, now felt tainted, its grandeur overshadowed by the shadow of Lucy Stow's murder and the subsequent revelations. The legal battles over the inheritance were far from over.

While Timothy was legally entitled to the estate, the social stigma associated with the scandal, the whispers and the sidelong glances from the local villagers, would inevitably cast a pall over his life. He contemplated selling the property, severing his ties with the past, but the idea felt like surrendering to the very forces that had attempted to destroy him. The weight of his heritage, the responsibility for the legacy of the Stow family, held him captive. He knew that selling Sheldon Hall would be acknowledging his defeat, a sign of surrender to the whispers and judgment that surrounded him. It was a heavy burden, a battle against not only the past but also the shadow of his own reputation.

Charles Stow, meanwhile, enjoyed a far less tumultuous aftermath, at least outwardly. He had escaped prosecution due to the clever loophole of double jeopardy, a legal technicality that Giallo had expertly exploited.

Yet, his triumph felt hollow. The guilt gnawed at him, even as he reveled in his newfound possession of the family fortune and the woman he loved. He had orchestrated a cruel and callous scheme, betraying not only Timothy, but also the memory of his deceased friend. The weight of his actions, the realization of the depth of his betrayal, proved a constant reminder of the true cost of his ambition. He looked upon Emily Grace with a mixture of love and guilt, her presence constantly whispering his dark deeds to him. Emily, too, felt the burden of their shared secret, the knowledge of their complicity in the death of Lucy Stow, the woman whose legacy they sought to plunder for their personal gain.

Their love was tarnished by the shadow of their crime, a constant reminder of the deceit that had driven them. Their stolen happiness was nothing more than a brittle trophy won through treachery.

The townspeople of the nearby village, initially captivated by the unfolding drama, now turned their gaze away from Sheldon Hall. The whispers surrounding the Stow family persisted, the truth revealed, but the underlying details of their actions, their motivations, had fueled a sense of disillusionment within the community. The narrative woven around this family, once considered the pillars of the community, now held a dark hue. Trust, once readily given, became a fragile commodity. The case of Lucy Stow's murder became a cautionary tale, a reminder of the unexpected twists and turns that life could take, a stark testament to the complexities of human nature.

Reeves Giallo, the quiet observer who had orchestrated the unraveling of the elaborate scheme, returned to his quiet life in York. The satisfaction of solving the case was tempered by the moral ambiguity of the outcome. He had exposed the truth, but justice, in its traditional sense, hadn't been served.

Charles Stow, the perpetrator, had walked free, a testament to the limitations of the law and the complexities of human justice. The case, however, had brought him a profound understanding of human nature, a deeper insight into the machinations of the human mind, a grim understanding of the dark side of human ambition. He documented the case, meticulously recording each detail, each twist and turn, each moment of revelation, aiming to create a detailed record of the case to understand the subtle intricacies of deceit and betrayal. The case served as both a triumph and a sobering reminder of the unpredictable nature of justice.

The aftermath of Lucy Stow's murder extended far beyond the courtroom and the confines of Sheldon Hall. It reverberated through the lives of those involved, leaving an indelible mark on the community and on the landscape of their lives. Timothy, forever bearing the scars of suspicion and loss, struggled to rebuild his life amid the ruins of his past. Charles and Emily, haunted by their actions, found their stolen happiness poisoned by guilt and the ever-present fear of exposure.

Inspector Marlow, shaken to the core, grappled with his redefined understanding of justice. Even Giallo, the detached observer, found himself affected by the moral complexities of the case. The shadow of Lucy Stow's murder, a dark stain on the tapestry of their lives, served as a poignant reminder that even in the aftermath of justice, the pursuit of truth remains a complex and ongoing process, a journey filled with ambiguity and unexpected turns, and that the truest form of justice often lies in the understanding of human nature rather than merely the observance of the law. The silent echoes of the case lingered, a haunting testament to the complexities of human nature, the subtle art of deception, and the often-elusive nature of true justice.

Sheldon Hall, once a symbol of family and tradition, remained a somber monument to the cost of ambition, betrayal, and the enduring mystery of the human heart. The winds continued to howl across the grounds, a constant reminder of the untold stories that whispered through the darkened hallways, echoing the ghosts of the past and the lingering uncertainty of the future. The case, while closed, would continue to resonate in the lives of those left behind, serving as a grim yet unforgettable lesson in the pursuit of truth and the complex, often unsatisfying, nature of justice.

The lingering silence was broken only by the whisper of the wind, as if lamenting the complexities of human nature and the enduring mystery of the human heart. The aftermath of the case of Lucy Stow's murder continued to unfold, not in the courtroom, but in the silent, shadowed spaces of the human soul.

CHAPTER 25
The Cost of Deception

The weight of their deception settled heavily upon Charles and Emily. The initial elation of escaping legal repercussions—the sweet taste of victory snatched from the jaws of defeat—quickly soured. Their meticulously crafted plan, a masterpiece of manipulation and deceit, had yielded the desired outcome: Sheldon Hall was theirs. But the manor, once a symbol of aspiration, now felt like a gilded cage, its grandeur overshadowed by the chilling reality of their actions. The opulent rooms, once filled with the promise of a shared future, echoed with the ghosts of their lies.

Emily, initially thrilled by the prospect of finally being with Charles, found herself increasingly tormented by guilt. The vibrant spark in her eyes, once alight with love and ambition, dimmed, replaced by a haunting uncertainty. She had participated in a cruel charade, sacrificing Timothy, a man she barely knew, at the altar of her desires. The weight of her complicity pressed down on her, manifesting in sleepless nights and a growing sense of isolation. The luxury that surrounded her felt less like a reward and more like a constant, suffocating reminder of her betrayal. Even Charles' presence, once a source of comfort and strength, now carried a tinge of unease. She saw in his eyes not only love, but also a chilling ruthlessness that had been hidden beneath a façade of charm and sensitivity.

Charles, initially confident in his cunning, found his carefully constructed world crumbling around him. The acquisition of Sheldon Hall, the fulfillment of his lifelong ambition, failed to bring him the satisfaction he craved. The shadow of Timothy's misfortune, the haunting image of a falsely accused man, lingered in his mind.

He had played God, manipulating the lives of others for his own gain, and the cost of his ambition was a profound and gnawing emptiness. He found himself increasingly withdrawn, haunted by the knowledge that the happiness he pursued was tainted, built on a foundation of lies and deceit. The grand estate, once a symbol of triumph, became a prison of his own making, its echoing halls a constant reminder of his moral failings. He discovered that the price of deception was far greater than the loss of potential freedom; it was the irrevocable loss of peace of mind, the perpetual shadow of guilt.

Timothy, exonerated but deeply scarred, struggled to find his footing in a world that had unjustly branded him a murderer. The ordeal had stripped him of his innocence and his trust in humanity. The initial relief at being cleared of the charges gave way to a profound sense of loss. He had lost his mother, his reputation, and his faith in those he once considered friends. The world, once perceived as a fair and just place, now appeared to him as a treacherous landscape of betrayal and deception. The social stigma clung to him like a second skin, making it difficult to rebuild his life and regain a sense of normalcy.

He withdrew from society, his once vibrant spirit dulled by the trauma he endured, forever haunted by the specter of false accusations. The legal victory was hollow, offering little solace in the face of his emotional wounds. His path to healing was long and arduous, a journey marked by sorrow, disillusionment, and the lingering pain of injustice.

Inspector Marlow, a man of unwavering integrity, found himself grappling with the unsettling implications of the case. He had witnessed firsthand the insidious nature of deception, its capacity to twist the truth into a grotesque parody of itself.

The carefully constructed web of lies woven by Charles and Emily shook his faith in the efficacy of justice, highlighting the limitations of the law in unmasking the complex machinations of the human heart.

He had pursued justice with unwavering dedication, but this case highlighted the inadequacy of the legal system in addressing the full spectrum of human motivations and the depth of human depravity. The experience left a profound mark on him, changing his perception of justice, reminding him that the law, while vital, offered only a partial and sometimes imperfect measure of truth. He understood that true justice went beyond legal pronouncements, residing in the restoration of integrity and the recognition of moral responsibility, a task which, in this case, felt impossible.

Reeves Giallo, the sharp and observant detective, whose intellect had cracked the case, carried his own burden. He possessed a detachment that enabled his keen observations, yet he found himself unable to remain completely unaffected by the emotional fallout. Witnessing the profound devastation caused by Charles and Emily's scheme highlighted the far-reaching and devastating consequences of deception. It was a lesson not solely in the techniques of detection, but in the depths of human depravity and the lasting impact of even the most cleverly crafted lies. The case underscored the devastating impact of unchecked ambition and the importance of moral responsibility.

Though he had exposed the truth, revealing the intricate tapestry of lies that led to Lucy Stow's untimely demise, he could not erase the pain inflicted. He realized that even the most complete victory couldn't fully compensate for the destruction wrought by deceit. The community of Sheldon Hall and its surrounding areas were irrevocably altered by the events surrounding Lucy Stow's murder.

The revelation of Charles and Emily's deceit shattered the veneer of respectability that had veiled their true motives. Gossip swirled like a noxious wind through the town, tainting reputations and fostering an atmosphere of suspicion and distrust. Social circles fractured, old friendships broken by the weight of unspoken accusations and hidden betrayals.

The tragic outcome cast a long shadow over the collective consciousness, a stark reminder of the fragility of trust and the corrosive impact of greed and ambition. The seemingly idyllic community was irrevocably altered, forever bearing the scars of a truth that had been concealed beneath layers of carefully crafted lies.

The aftermath of the case served as a stark warning, a chilling testament to the cost of deception. It was not merely the legal ramifications, the potential imprisonment, or the social ostracism that mattered, but the profound erosion of moral integrity, the irreversible damage done to relationships, and the enduring weight of guilt. Charles and Emily, though seemingly triumphant, were condemned to live with the consequences of their actions — a punishment far more severe than any prison sentence.

Their stolen happiness would be forever tainted by the shadow of their deceit. Their actions served as a cautionary tale, a poignant illustration of how the pursuit of personal gain, fuelled by unchecked ambition, could lead to unforeseen and devastating consequences. The case of Lucy Stow's murder echoed beyond the confines of Sheldon Hall, serving as a somber reminder that the price of deception is far greater than any fleeting reward. The echoes of their actions served as a constant reminder of the enduring power of truth and the devastating cost of betrayal.

The legacy of Lucy Stow's death was not a simple matter of justice served, but a complicated tapestry woven with the threads of guilt, regret, and the enduring shadow of deception. In the quiet aftermath, the true cost of their actions became painfully clear: the irrevocable damage done to their souls, and the lasting imprint of their betrayal on those around them.

The story of Lucy Stow's murder, while ostensibly resolved, would continue to resonate through the lives of those it touched, a constant reminder of the complexities of human nature, the alluring power of deception, and the devastating consequences of prioritizing personal gain over moral integrity.

CHAPTER 26
Sheldon Halls Future

The dust motes danced in the late afternoon sunbeams slanting through the tall windows of Sheldon Hall. The air, once thick with the suffocating weight of suspicion and death, now held a fragile stillness, a quietude that felt both earned and precarious. The grand house, a silent witness to the unraveling of secrets and lies, seemed to breathe a sigh of relief. Timothy Stow, exonerated but still bearing the scars of wrongful accusation, stood on the terrace, gazing at the meticulously kept gardens. The vibrant colors, a stark contrast to the somber hues that had dominated his life for the past few months, offered a tentative promise of spring.

Sheldon Hall, once a symbol of inherited privilege and suffocating family dynamics, now held a different weight. The shadow of Lucy Stow's murder, a dark stain upon its history, lingered, but the truth, like a stubborn weed pushing through the carefully manicured lawn, had finally broken through the surface. The meticulous investigation, culminating in the arrest of Charles and Emily, had stripped away the carefully constructed façade of respectability, revealing the raw, ugly truth of greed and betrayal. The house, once a testament to the Stow family's wealth and standing, now felt oddly vulnerable, its future uncertain.

The immediate future was clear: the legal battles would continue. The intricacies of the will, previously a source of contention and manipulation, would now be untangled under the watchful eye of the courts. Charles and Emily's assets, once the object of their avarice, would be carefully assessed and distributed, a process that promised further upheaval and strained relationships.

However, Timothy, despite the trauma he endured, was resolute in his decision. He wouldn't let the tainted legacy of his mother and the actions of his cousin and supposed friend destroy the family name entirely. He intended to restore the Stow name, not by clinging to the past, but by forging a new path, one built on honesty and transparency.

He planned to sell Sheldon Hall. The decision was not made lightly. The house held too many memories, both good and bad. But it was also a physical embodiment of the deceit and manipulation that had cost his mother her life and nearly ruined his. It represented a past he couldn't, and wouldn't, run from, but one he also couldn't afford to be tethered to any longer. The proceeds from the sale would allow him to start anew, somewhere far from the suffocating shadows of Sheldon Hall, a place where he could rebuild his life without the constant reminder of the tragedy. He would use some of the money to establish a charitable foundation, aiming to support war veterans struggling with their transition back to civilian life, a cause close to his heart, given his own experiences and his recent brush with injustice. It would be a fitting tribute to Lucy, a woman who, despite her flaws, possessed a surprising depth of compassion.

The departure of Charles and Emily left a void in the estate, both literally and figuratively. The staff, long accustomed to the machinations of the Stow family, were left to adjust to a new reality. There were whispers of relief, of course, but also a sense of unease. The future of their employment remained uncertain, hanging in the balance like a fragile pendulum.

But Timothy, in a gesture of unexpected kindness, assured them that their positions would remain secure, at least during the transition period. He understood that they were not complicit in the crimes; they were victims, too, of the family's poisonous dynamics.

Reeves Giallo, the quiet observer, the mastermind behind the unraveling of the intricate web of deceit, watched the changes unfold with a detached yet empathetic gaze. He had seen the darkness within the human heart, the depths to which ambition and greed could drive people. The case had taken a significant toll on him, a reminder that even the most meticulous investigations could not completely sanitize the wounds left by betrayal.

Yet, he found a strange sense of satisfaction in bringing justice to Lucy Stow, even if it came at a considerable personal cost. The quiet satisfaction of a case well-solved was tempered by the sobering reminder of the human capacity for cruelty. He recognized that Sheldon Hall was not simply a building, but a microcosm of society, revealing its complexities and contradictions.

Inspector Marlow, his reputation slightly tarnished but his integrity intact, accepted Giallo's explanation of the case with a grudging respect. He had been too quick to judge, blinded by the surface appearances and the pressure to bring a swift closure to the case. The encounter with Giallo, and the unveiling of the elaborate scheme, had forced him to reassess his investigative methods.

He understood that sometimes, the most obvious answer was not always the correct one, and that beneath the veneer of polite society lay a dark underbelly of secrets and deceptions. He resolved to approach future investigations with a greater sense of caution and a more nuanced understanding of human nature.

The epilogue of the Sheldon Hall tragedy wasn't simply a closing chapter but a reflection on the enduring power of human nature. The tale of Charles and Emily's downfall served as a cautionary reminder of the destructive force of greed and the lengths to which people would go to achieve their desires. It was a testament to the importance of truth, the resilience of the human spirit, and the complex interplay between justice and forgiveness.

The mystery wasn't just about solving a murder; it was about understanding the motivations behind it, the intricate web of relationships, and the lasting impact of deception.

Timothy, having escaped the clutches of a manipulative scheme, began to rebuild his life. He moved to a small cottage near the coast, finding solace in the rhythm of the waves and the solitude of the sea. He established his charitable foundation, dedicating his time and resources to helping others, particularly war veterans. The work brought a sense of purpose and fulfillment, allowing him to channel his grief and trauma into something positive and meaningful.

His association with Sheldon Hall, once a source of shame and sorrow, evolved into a distant memory, replaced by the fresh hope and anticipation of a new beginning.

The sale of Sheldon Hall itself marked a significant turning point. The new owners, a young couple, had plans to transform the manor into a center for arts and culture, opening it up to the public. It was a fitting transformation, a symbolic shift from a house steeped in secrecy and family discord to a space that would promote creativity and community. This act represented not just the end of an era for the Stow family, but also a fresh start for Sheldon Hall, suggesting that even from tragedy and destruction, beauty and rejuvenation can arise.

The house, once haunted by ghosts of the past, was now infused with the promise of a vibrant future, a testament to the resilience of life. The memory of Lucy Stow, while never truly fading, would be less a symbol of familial conflict, but more of a catalyst for change, a poignant reminder that even in the face of betrayal and injustice, hope persists.

Giallo, however, continued his work as a detective, his sharp mind ever vigilant, his keen eye always searching for the subtle clues that concealed the truth. He had learned that every case was a new puzzle, a testament to the unpredictable nature of human behavior. Sheldon Hall, with its intricate secrets and twisted relationships, left an indelible mark on him.

It reminded him that beneath the surface of polished manners and societal expectations, darker forces often lurked. His experiences at Sheldon Hall refined his understanding of human nature, shaping him into a more experienced, insightful, and even compassionate investigator. His future cases would undoubtedly benefit from his encounter with the complex dynamics within the walls of Sheldon Hall.

The enduring mystery of human nature, the unpredictable twists and turns of life, remained. Sheldon Hall's legacy would continue to resonate, a poignant reminder that the past, even when buried deep, often has a way of resurfacing.

But it was also a testament to the resilience of the human spirit, a celebration of justice, and a powerful reflection on the ongoing struggle between truth and deception. The closing of one chapter in Sheldon Hall's history did not necessarily signify the end of its story, but rather, the beginning of a new, less turbulent, and hopefully, more hopeful era for all those touched by its events. The house stood, silent yet powerful, a witness to both tragedy and hope, the echoes of its past whispering promises of the future.

CHAPTER 27
Giallo's Reflections

The scent of woodsmoke and damp earth clung to my coat, a lingering reminder of Sheldon Hall and the unsettling game of deception that had played out within its walls. The case was closed, the guilty exposed, justice, in a twisted fashion, served. Yet, as I sat in the dimly lit carriage, the rhythmic clatter of the wheels against the cobblestones a counterpoint to the turmoil in my mind, the echoes of the Stow family tragedy resonated far louder than the celebratory clinking of glasses I imagined back at the manor. It wasn't the simple satisfaction of solving a complex puzzle that lingered; it was the unsettling weight of human fallibility, the chilling ease with which truth could be obscured, and the devastating consequences that followed.

This case, more than most, had peeled back the layers of societal veneer, revealing the raw, often ugly, truths lurking beneath. The veneer of respectability that cloaked the Stow family had crumbled, revealing a nest of greed, betrayal, and desperation. Charles, the seemingly grieving friend, the composed heir, had been a master manipulator, orchestrating a plot so intricate, so audacious, that even I, with my years of experience, had been nearly misled. His love for Emily, a love so fierce it blinded him to the moral abyss he was plunging into, was a potent, terrifying force. It was a love that justified the calculated cruelty, the cold-blooded murder, the callous disregard for the life of Lucy Stow.

And Timothy? The initial suspect, the son burdened by a dubious alibi, the man whose despair had been palpable, was ultimately a victim, a pawn in a game orchestrated by those he considered family. His naivety, his trust, had been cruelly exploited, leaving him scarred, his innocence tarnished by the mudslinging of a carefully constructed falsehood. He had lost his mother, his reputation, and a considerable portion of his inheritance, all stolen by the very people he trusted most.

The legal system, while ultimately just, had failed to fully account for the emotional wreckage left in its wake. Timothy's future, shrouded in the shadow of suspicion, would bear the weight of this injustice for a long time to come.

Emily Grace, the seemingly demure cousin, proved herself to be a surprisingly capable accomplice, her intelligence and resourcefulness equal to Charles' ambition. Her participation, however, painted a more complex portrait.

Was it love that drove her, a blind loyalty to Charles, or was there a deeper ambition at play, a desire for power and wealth that mirrored Charles' own? Her silence, even after the truth was revealed, suggested a lingering complicity, a reluctance to fully expose the depth of their collusion. The unspoken questions, the unanswered nuances, hung in the air like a persistent fog, refusing to dissipate even after the storm had passed.

Inspector Marlow, a man of routine and procedure, had almost fallen victim to the carefully laid traps. His reliance on immediate, readily available evidence had led him down a path of misplaced certainty, a path that could have resulted in a terrible miscarriage of justice. The case served as a stark reminder of the limitations of even the most diligent investigations; that the most obvious answer is not always the correct one, and that the pursuit of justice requires a sharper eye, a deeper understanding of human nature, and an unwavering commitment to truth, no matter how inconvenient it may be.

The letter, the pivotal piece of evidence, the confession disguised as a testament to love, was a testament to Charles' audacity.

It was a calculated risk, a gamble on his ability to manipulate not just the people around him, but the very fabric of truth itself. The letter's existence underscored the ease with which words could be used to construct intricate webs of lies, to manipulate emotions, and to ultimately justify heinous actions.

This case transcended the simple confines of a murder investigation; it was a study in the fragility of human relationships, the corrosive power of greed, and the enduring resilience of the human spirit. It revealed the intricate dance between truth and deception, a dance in which the steps are rarely clear, the music often discordant, and the outcome always uncertain. The meticulous collection of evidence, the painstaking analysis of facts, and the careful piecing together of seemingly unrelated details — these were not just aspects of my profession; they were essential tools for navigating the labyrinthine world of human interaction, a world where the appearance of reality often obscures the harsh truth. The experience left me with a profound sense of unease, a lingering shadow cast by the darkness I had encountered.

The faces of the Stows, their expressions ranging from calculated composure to desperate despair, continued to haunt my waking hours. I saw the reflection of their choices in the eyes of others, in the subtle shifts in demeanor, in the hesitant smiles. The case became a mirror reflecting not only their actions, but the potential for similar darkness within us all. It was a reminder that the line between good and evil is often blurred, that human nature is a complex tapestry woven with threads of both light and shadow.

Beyond the courtroom victory, beyond the exoneration of Timothy, lay a deeper, more profound contemplation. The investigation had exposed the inherent risks in blind faith, in the unquestioning acceptance of perceived truths, and in the insidious nature of unchecked ambition.

The case challenged the very foundations of trust, reminding me of the importance of critical thinking, of the need to question, to probe, to delve beneath the surface before arriving at any conclusions. The ability to see beyond the façade, to recognize the subtle cues, the carefully constructed narratives, the deliberate omissions – these were the skills that had ultimately led to the resolution of the case, skills honed not merely through deductive reasoning, but through years of observation, empathy, and a deep understanding of the human condition.

The aftermath at Sheldon Hall was a strange mix of relief and profound unease. The house, once a stage for tragedy, now seemed to exhale, the weight of secrets lifted from its ancient stones. Yet, the very silence that followed the storm was somehow more disturbing than the cacophony of accusations and suspicions that had preceded it. The lingering scent of fear, of betrayal, of death, clung to the air, a chilling reminder of the depths of human depravity that had been exposed. The vibrant colors of the gardens, once a symbol of hope, now felt strangely muted, their beauty overshadowed by the haunting memory of Lucy Stow's lifeless body.

The case of Lucy Stow's murder served as a grim reminder of the fragility of life and the enduring power of deception. It highlighted the importance of meticulous investigation, not merely as a means of solving crimes, but as a way of understanding the complexities of human nature, the subtle nuances of motivation, and the devastating consequences of unchecked ambition. The unraveling of the truth, while satisfying, left a residue of unsettling questions, a lingering sense of unease that echoed the quiet desperation of those left in its wake. The journey back to York was filled with introspection.

The case wasn't simply about solving a murder; it was about confronting the darkness that lurks within us all, the capacity for betrayal, the seductive allure of power, and the enduring struggle between truth and deception. It was a journey into the heart of human nature, a journey that left me profoundly changed, forever marked by the shadows and the unsettling echoes of Sheldon Hall.

The experience underscored the responsibility of those who seek justice, the necessity of unwavering integrity, and the enduring importance of truth in a world often shrouded in lies. The quiet hum of the carriage, the rhythmic clatter of the wheels, became a melancholic soundtrack to my reflections, a testament to the enduring mysteries of human nature and the persistent struggle between light and shadow. The case was closed, but the lessons learned, the questions pondered, and the lingering unease remained, etched indelibly in the chambers of my mind, a haunting reminder of the darkness that even the brightest light can fail to fully dispel.

CHAPTER 28
Lessons Learned

The carriage lurched, throwing me against the worn leather of the seat. The jarring movement jolted me from my reverie, from the swirling vortex of deceit and betrayal that had consumed me for weeks. The case of Lucy Stow's murder was closed, the perpetrators exposed, but the unsettling residue of the experience clung to me like the persistent York fog. It wasn't just the solving of a crime; it was the stark revelation of human nature, a chilling glimpse into the abyss of ambition and the seductive power of lies.

Sheldon Hall, once a symbol of stately elegance, now stood in my memory as a mausoleum of secrets, its polished floors reflecting the distorted images of those who inhabited its walls. Charles Stow, initially appearing as a grieving friend, had revealed himself to be a calculating manipulator, his grief a carefully constructed mask concealing a ruthless ambition. His love for Emily Grace, his cousin, was real enough, but it was a love twisted by avarice, fueled by the desire for wealth and status. Their elaborate scheme, a tapestry woven with carefully placed clues and cleverly orchestrated events, had almost succeeded. Only my relentless pursuit of truth, my refusal to accept convenient explanations, had unravelled their carefully constructed web of deception.

The irony wasn't lost on me. Justice, in this instance, had been served in a most peculiar manner. Timothy Stow, the initial prime suspect, had been exonerated, not through a triumphant unveiling of his innocence, but through the exposure of his parents' perfidy. He was left not with the satisfaction of vindication, but with the shattering realization that his mother's death was a consequence of his own family's cruel machinations. The legal system, with its rigid procedures and adherence to the letter of the law, had been circumvented by the clever manipulation of its very principles. The double jeopardy clause, meant to protect the innocent from repeated prosecution, had been exploited as a weapon by the guilty, a testament to the vulnerability of even the most carefully crafted legal frameworks.

This case underscored a profound truth: the law, while a vital instrument of justice, is not infallible. It is a tool, a framework, but its effectiveness hinges on the integrity and diligence of those who wield it. Inspector Marlow, for all his experience and dedication, had been almost entirely misled. He had relied on superficial evidence, on appearances, and had been blinded by the carefully constructed façade presented by Charles and Emily. It was only through the meticulous examination of seemingly insignificant details, through the persistent questioning of assumptions, that the truth had emerged.

The lessons learned extended beyond the specific circumstances of the Stow case. It was a stark reminder of the corrosive power of greed, the destructive nature of unchecked ambition, and the insidious ways in which deceit can infiltrate even the most seemingly stable relationships. The bond between Charles and Emily, initially perceived as a testament to love's resilience, was revealed to be a toxic cocktail of passion and avarice. Their love, it seemed, was as much about the acquisition of power and wealth as it was about emotional connection.

This raised a disquieting question: how can one truly differentiate between genuine affection and the manipulative guise of love? Where does the line blur between genuine emotion and calculated self-interest?
The investigation into Lucy Stow's death had forced me to confront the darker aspects of human nature, the capacity for betrayal that lurks beneath the surface of even the most respectable facades. The elegant drawing rooms of

Sheldon Hall had concealed a viper's nest of secrets, whispered conversations masking callous intentions, and carefully crafted smiles concealing deep-seated malice. The experience left me profoundly disturbed, forcing me to question the reliability of appearances and the fragility of trust. The case was not a simple triumph of detection; it was a descent into the murky depths of human depravity, a stark reminder of the chasm that can separate appearance from reality.

Yet, amidst the darkness, there was a glimmer of hope. The ultimate revelation of the truth, the exposure of Charles and Emily's scheme, served as a testament to the enduring power of justice. While the legal system may have been manipulated, the truth, however inconvenient, eventually prevailed. It was a victory, albeit a bittersweet one, highlighting the importance of unwavering integrity, the relentless pursuit of facts, and the courage to confront even the most uncomfortable truths. The meticulous process of deduction, the painstaking analysis of evidence, the unwavering pursuit of the truth – these were the tools that ultimately shattered the meticulously crafted illusion of innocence and exposed the cruel reality of the Stow family's dark secret.

The journey back to York was not merely a physical transition; it was a journey of introspection, a process of sifting through the complexities of the case, absorbing the lessons it had imparted. The rhythmic clatter of the carriage wheels against the cobblestones served as a constant reminder of the relentless pursuit of justice, a journey marked by twists, turns, and unexpected revelations. The case, while closed, continued to resonate within me, a constant reminder of the deceptive nature of appearances and the enduring struggle between light and shadow. I had seen the darkness firsthand, witnessed the extent of human depravity, and yet I found myself clinging to a renewed faith in the enduring power of truth.

Even when obscured by lies and carefully constructed facades, the truth always finds a way to emerge. It's a slow, painstaking process sometimes, but it is a process that is ultimately unyielding.

The lingering unease, the unsettling echoes of Sheldon Hall, would undoubtedly remain with me. But it was an unease tempered by a profound understanding – an understanding not just of the methods of deception and the intricacies of criminal investigation, but of the darker corners of human nature, the fragility of trust, and the enduring importance of truth. The case had left an indelible mark on my soul, altering my perspective, sharpening my instincts, and solidifying my resolve to pursue justice, however elusive it may sometimes seem.

The lessons learned were not simply technical observations but profound insights into the human condition, shaping not only my methods as a detective but also my understanding of the world around me.

The experience served as a potent reminder that justice is not always served in neat and tidy packages. It is a messy, complicated affair, often shrouded in ambiguity and marked by unexpected twists. The path to truth is rarely straightforward; it requires patience, perseverance, and a keen eye for detail. The Stow case had tested my limits, challenged my assumptions, and pushed me to the very edge of my capabilities. And yet, in its aftermath, I found myself both exhausted and exhilarated, profoundly changed by the lessons learned and forever marked by the shadows and unsettling echoes of Sheldon Hall.

The knowledge gained, the skills honed, and the profound insights into the human condition were rewards in themselves, far outweighing any personal triumph or professional recognition. The case had redefined my understanding of justice, truth, and the human capacity for both extraordinary good and unimaginable evil.

The rhythmic clatter of the carriage continued, the monotonous sound a counterpoint to the chaotic symphony of thoughts and emotions that swirled within me. The journey back to York was a journey of reflection, a silent testament to the mysteries of human nature and the enduring struggle between light and shadow.

The city lights, shimmering in the distance, promised a return to normalcy, but I knew that a part of me would always remain at Sheldon Hall, haunted by the shadows of the past, forever shaped by the lessons learned in the aftermath of Lucy Stow's tragic death. The case was closed, but the echoes of the past, the whispers of deceit and the weight of the truth, would forever remain, a constant reminder of the complexities of human nature and the relentless pursuit of justice.

The road ahead was long, and the mysteries to be solved were numerous, but I knew, with a certainty that went beyond mere confidence, that I would carry the lessons learned from Sheldon Hall with me, always. The journey may be solitary, the work arduous, but the pursuit of truth, however challenging, was a journey I was now forever committed to.

CHAPTER 29
A New Beginning for Timothy

The carriage wheels crunched on the gravel driveway, a stark contrast to the hushed silence that had settled over Sheldon Hall in the wake of the scandal. The air, once thick with suspicion and the cloying scent of deceit, now held a fragile lightness, a tentative peace. Timothy, released from the suffocating grip of suspicion, stepped onto the grounds, his shoulders no longer slumped with the weight of false accusation. He looked back at the imposing manor, a place that had become synonymous with betrayal, yet now, oddly, with a sense of liberation. It was a strange feeling, this mix of relief and lingering unease. The ordeal had stripped him bare, exposed his vulnerability, and left him questioning the very foundations of his life.

He had been exonerated, yes, but the shadow of the accusation still lingered. He knew that the whispers would persist, some fuelled by lingering doubt, others by the inherent human tendency to relish a good scandal. But he also knew that Reeves Giallo's meticulous investigation had spoken volumes. The truth, however bitter its unveiling, had finally been heard. The weight of the false accusations had been lifted, but the emotional scars remained – a constant reminder of the fragility of justice and the venomous power of lies. The experience had, in a way, hardened him, sharpened his senses to the subtle nuances of deceit. He had witnessed firsthand how easily a fabricated narrative could ensnare even the most innocent. But it had also tempered him, imbuing him with an unwavering resolve to seek out the truth, regardless of the cost.

The future stretched before him, vast and uncertain, yet brimming with potential. The family fortune, once a source of conflict and contention, was now a catalyst for a new beginning. He hadn't inherited the estate, not in the way that had been initially planned, but the financial security it afforded him offered a degree of freedom he hadn't anticipated. He had the means now to pursue his own path, to build a life independent of the shadows that had once cloaked Sheldon Hall. He envisioned a future where he could dedicate himself to pursuits he had once only dreamed of – perhaps a life of travel, a chance to see the world beyond the confines of the English countryside, a world that had seemed so distant during his imprisonment in the web of deceit.

His thoughts drifted to Inspector Marlow, a man who, despite his initial suspicions, had shown a surprising degree of fairness once presented with the irrefutable evidence.

Timothy hadn't forgotten Marlow's initial skepticism, the hard glint in his eyes during the interrogation. But Marlow, bound by duty to follow the law, had also demonstrated a capacity for understanding once the truth emerged. Their parting had been quiet, marked by a mutual acknowledgment of the complexities of the case and a tacit understanding of the burdens borne by both sides. There was no need for apologies, no need for resentment. They had both fulfilled their respective roles within a complex framework of justice, a framework that, while imperfect, had ultimately served its purpose.

Timothy's gaze settled upon the sprawling grounds of Sheldon Hall. The gardens, once a stage for clandestine meetings and hushed conversations, now held only the promise of new growth. He saw a future where he could plant new seeds, nurture new beginnings, and cultivate a different landscape, one devoid of the bitterness and betrayal that had marred the past.

The stately home, looming in the background, would always be a reminder of this chapter of his life, a chapter filled with darkness, yet leading to an unexpected dawn. He considered approaching the house, perhaps to pay a final farewell to the place that had been both his prison and, in a strange twist of fate, the catalyst for his emancipation. But the need to linger felt unnecessary.

The future, he realized, lay not behind him, within the walls of Sheldon Hall, but stretched ahead, towards the horizon, beckoning him with possibilities yet to be discovered.

The journey to York was a quiet contemplation, a meditation on the past few months. He reflected on the relationships that had been fractured, the bonds that had been tested, and the unexpected alliances that had emerged during the tumultuous events. Charles Stow, his cousin, remained a man of contradictions – capable of both profound cruelty and surprising acts of kindness. Timothy felt no desire for revenge; rather, a weary sense of pity. Charles' actions had been motivated by greed and a desperate desire for security, a warped reflection of the anxieties of the war-torn world.

His misguided attempts to secure his future had nearly destroyed Timothy's life, and that thought, above all, instilled in him a profound sense of sadness.
Emily Grace, the enigmatic cousin who had played such a pivotal role in the scheme, occupied a space in his thoughts as complex as the woman herself. Her presence at Sheldon Hall had been both a source of comfort and bewilderment. Her apparent involvement in the plot, however disturbing, had never truly seemed like a deliberate act of malice. Her motivation remained unclear even after the revelation of Charles' letter; a mystery that perhaps would never be fully unraveled. The nuances of her actions were lost in the shadow of larger events.

Reeves Giallo, the shrewd detective whose intellect and persistence had brought the truth to light, was a true beacon during his darkest hour. His relentless pursuit of justice, his unwavering belief in the power of observation and deduction, had restored Timothy's faith in the integrity of the human spirit.

The detective's quiet demeanor had provided a calming influence amidst the chaos, his methodical approach a stark contrast to the frantic efforts of others. He was a man of few words, but his actions spoke volumes, offering a silent testament to his dedication to justice.

The carriage pulled to a stop in York, its arrival marking a transition from the claustrophobic world of Sheldon Hall to the bustling anonymity of the city. The familiar sights and sounds of York, once monotonous, now held a sense of renewed wonder. The bustling streets, the distant sounds of church bells, the vibrant energy of the city – it was a life reborn. He walked away from the carriage, leaving behind not only the physical confines of Sheldon Hall, but also the emotional baggage that had weighed heavily on him. The city's hum and energy offered a new rhythm, a new pace. This was his new beginning.

The days that followed were filled with a sense of cautious optimism. Timothy found himself drawn to activities that offered a respite from the past – long walks along the River Ouse, visits to museums and galleries, and evenings spent reading literature that had been neglected during his ordeal.

He sought solace in quiet introspection, allowing himself time to process the events that had unfolded and to begin healing. The initial stages of recovery were slow and deliberate, a steady process of rebuilding his life and restoring his faith in human nature.

He began exploring his newfound freedom. The financial security afforded by his mother's will, once a source of contention, was now a tool for self-discovery. He enrolled in evening classes, rekindling an interest in history that had been dormant for years. He discovered a talent for drawing, a hidden passion he had never explored. He started to cultivate new relationships, forming friendships with fellow students and colleagues who showed him that trust and loyalty were still possible despite the betrayal he had endured. His interactions with these individuals instilled in him a faith in humanity, restoring a hope that had seemed lost after the ordeal at Sheldon Hall.

He also sought out Reeves Giallo, eager to express his gratitude and to maintain the unexpected friendship that had blossomed amidst the shadows of the investigation. Their meetings were punctuated by the quiet exchange of stories and insights, a camaraderie born of shared experiences and a mutual respect for the complexities of human behaviour.

Giallo, ever the astute observer, noticed the shift in Timothy's demeanor, the newfound confidence that radiated from him. Their conversations often ranged beyond the case itself, delving into broader societal issues and the enduring struggle between justice and injustice. The companionship and mentorship offered by the detective provided a lifeline, a sense of guidance as Timothy navigated the unfamiliar waters of his new beginning.

Timothy found solace in the routine of his new life, a life he had carefully constructed, brick by painstaking brick. The memories of Sheldon Hall remained, but they were no longer shackles binding him to the past. They were instead lessons learned, scars that bore testament to his resilience and his capacity for redemption. His future, once shrouded in uncertainty, was now a canvas upon which he was free to paint his own masterpiece.

It was a future filled with hope, a future where he could rewrite his own narrative, a narrative marked not by betrayal and despair, but by resilience, self-discovery, and the unwavering pursuit of a life well-lived.

He had emerged from the shadows of Sheldon Hall, transformed, stronger, and ready to embrace a new beginning, a testament to the enduring human spirit's capacity for healing and growth. His journey was a testament to the resilience of the human spirit and the power of hope amidst adversity. He carried the weight of the past, but he was no longer defined by it. He was Timothy, reborn.

CHAPTER 30
The Enduring Mystery of Human Nature

The gravel crunched under Timothy's boots, a sound strangely comforting after the echoing silence of the interrogation room, the suffocating weight of false accusations. He hadn't returned to Sheldon Hall. The very sight of the imposing manor, once a symbol of family and security, now evoked a chilling sense of betrayal, a stark reminder of the intricate web of deceit that had nearly consumed him. He had chosen a small cottage, nestled in York's countryside on Old York Road, far from the opulent grandeur of his former life, far from the shadows that clung to the memory of Sheldon Hall. It was a deliberate choice, a conscious distancing from the past.

He found himself pondering the events that had transpired, the intricate machinations of Charles and Emily, their carefully constructed plot to secure the Stow fortune. Their actions had revealed a darkness he hadn't anticipated, a callous disregard for his well-being, a ruthlessness that went beyond simple greed. It wasn't just the theft of his inheritance, but the deliberate attempt to ruin his life, to cast him as a murderer in the eyes of society. The betrayal stung, a deep wound that time wouldn't easily heal. Yet, even amidst the pain, a flicker of understanding ignited. He couldn't fully comprehend the depths of their ambition, but he could acknowledge the disturbing capacity for manipulation inherent in human nature.

Charles, his mentor, the man he had once considered a father figure, was capable of such cruelty. Emily, a woman who had seemed so refined, so elegant, had played her part in this elaborate charade with cold calculation. Their actions raised profound questions about the nature of relationships, the inherent fragility of trust. How could he have been so blind to the deceit that simmered beneath the surface of their polite interactions? How could he have missed the warning signs? The answer was both simple and unsettling: he hadn't wanted to see them. He had been blinded by the comfort of familiar ties, by the ingrained belief in the goodness of those he knew.

The investigation, conducted with meticulous detail by Reeves Giallo, had unearthed a tapestry of lies, a labyrinth of deception. Giallo's insight, his relentless pursuit of the truth, had been crucial. He had seen through the carefully constructed façade, the expertly planted evidence, recognizing the subtle inconsistencies, the carefully concealed motives. Giallo's dedication wasn't just about solving a murder; it was about unveiling the darker side of human nature, the unsettling capacity for betrayal that lurked within the seemingly respectable circles of society. This capacity wasn't confined to the wealthy or powerful; it existed within families, within friendships, within the closest of bonds.

The trial, though short-lived due to the revelation of Charles' letter, had been a harrowing experience. The glare of the public eye, the judgmental whispers, the relentless scrutiny – all of it had taken its toll. He'd felt the sting of suspicion, the suffocating pressure of being wrongly accused. The experience had been a brutal lesson in the fallibility of justice and the biases that can cloud even the most astute minds. Inspector Marlow, for example, had been quick to assume guilt, letting preconceived notions guide his judgment. He hadn't fully considered Timothy's character, dismissing his protests as mere attempts at evasion.

The ordeal had forced Timothy to confront not only the actions of others, but also his own shortcomings. He had been naïve, trusting, perhaps even foolish in his assumptions.

He had failed to recognize the subtle signs of deception, the carefully masked ambitions lurking beneath the surface of polite conversation. He had allowed his own ingrained sense of trust to blind him to the darker aspects of human nature.

Now, however, he was different. The experience had changed him fundamentally, instilling a newfound awareness of the complexities of human behavior, a cautionary understanding of the unpredictable nature of relationships.

He found solace in his work, restoring old manuscripts in the quiet solitude of his cottage. The delicate task of preserving the past gave him a sense of purpose, a grounding that the chaos of Sheldon Hall had denied him. Each carefully mended page was a small victory, a symbol of rebuilding, a tangible representation of his own journey towards healing.

The work was methodical, demanding patience and precision, qualities that had been sorely tested during his ordeal. It was therapeutic, allowing him to channel his emotions into a creative outlet, converting the pain of betrayal into a constructive endeavor.

He often found himself contemplating the letter, the piece of evidence that had finally shattered the carefully constructed facade of Charles and Emily's deceit. It wasn't just the content of the letter – the confession of their plan – that was significant; it was the very existence of the letter, the deliberate act of writing down their intentions, the chilling realization that their actions were premeditated, coldly calculated. This deliberate act underscored the terrifying potential for premeditation in human nature, the capacity for meticulously planned cruelty. It was a reminder that evil often isn't impulsive; it's deliberate, planned, and meticulously executed.

His thoughts drifted back to Lucy Stow, her unexpected death the catalyst for this entire chain of events. He had known her only briefly, yet her passing had unleashed a torrent of hidden emotions and long-buried resentments. Had her death been a mere coincidence, a tragic accident, or had deeper, darker forces been at play? Even with the truth exposed, a lingering sense of uncertainty remained. He couldn't completely shake the feeling that there were still unanswered questions, untold stories, hidden motives that remained shrouded in mystery.

The enduring mystery wasn't just about Lucy Stow's murder; it was about the enduring mystery of human nature itself. It was about the capacity for both great love and profound betrayal, the perplexing duality of the human heart. It was about the intricate web of relationships, the delicate balance of trust and suspicion, the unpredictable twists and turns of fate. It was about the enduring questions that plagued humanity: the ability to deceive, to manipulate, to inflict pain, all while maintaining a façade of normalcy and respectability.

He often wondered about Charles and Emily, about their lives after the scandal, the consequences they faced for their actions. He knew they would carry the weight of their guilt, the burden of their deceit. He did not harbor resentment, but a certain understanding of their flaws. He couldn't condone their actions, but he could comprehend the dark desires that had driven them. Their actions stood as a testament to the unpredictable nature of ambition and the devastating consequences that often result when greed and deception intertwine.

Timothy found a strange sort of peace in the quiet of his rural life, a peace born not of ignorance but of understanding. He had learned a profound lesson about human nature, a lesson that was both disturbing and enlightening.

He understood that the world wasn't always fair, that justice wasn't always swift, and that the darker aspects of humanity could emerge even in the most unexpected places. The experience had hardened him, sharpened his perception, but it had also strengthened his resolve, his capacity for compassion, and his unwavering belief in the resilience of the human spirit.

The enduring mystery of human nature would always be a source of both fascination and apprehension, yet it was a mystery that he was now better equipped to navigate. He had survived Sheldon Hall, but more importantly, he had survived the darkness within himself and others. He had found his own strength, forged in the fires of betrayal and injustice, a strength that would sustain him in the years to come. He was Timothy, reborn, and his future, though not without its shadows, was now brightly illuminated with the promise of a new dawn.

REEVES WILL FACE MORE TURMOIL IN BOOK THREE OF "REEVES GIALLO'S DETECTIVE SERIES "

WATCH FOR IT, COMING SOON

~ ~ ~

I hope you enjoyed *Murder at Sheldon Hall.* If you did, it would be a *GREAT* help to me if you told your friends. The lifeblood of a book is word of mouth and reviews. It would help me a lot if you left an honest review online so others will know what you thought about Reeves Giallo's detective stories.

Go to an online bookseller and leave a review and tell your family and friends. Thank you so much for your support. There are many more books about our famous detective Adventures coming soon.

www.ingramcontent.com/pod-product-compliance
Lightning Source LLC
LaVergne TN
LVHW020005260125
802063LV00024B/915